SUSPENDED

SUSPENDED

S. L. HEMM

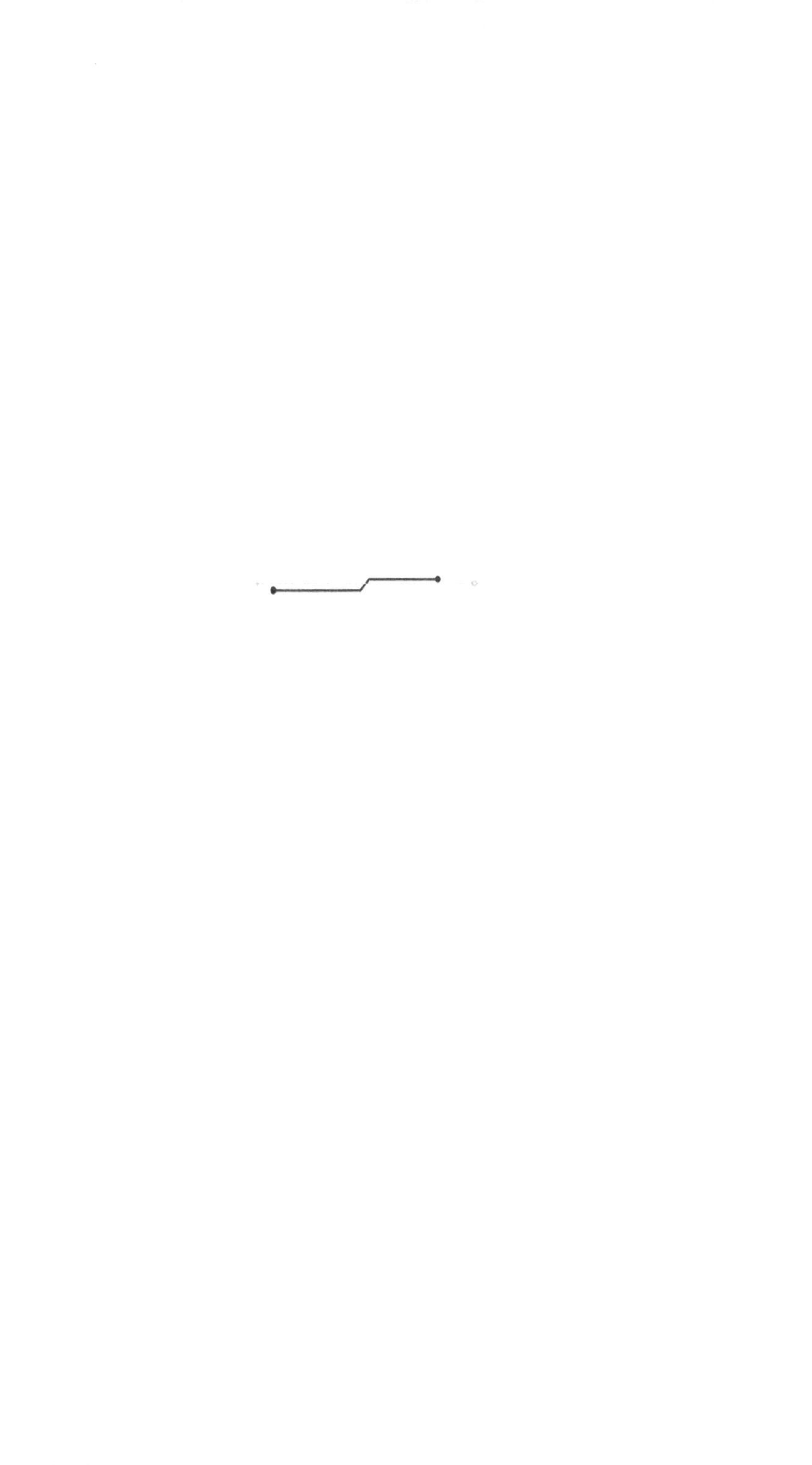

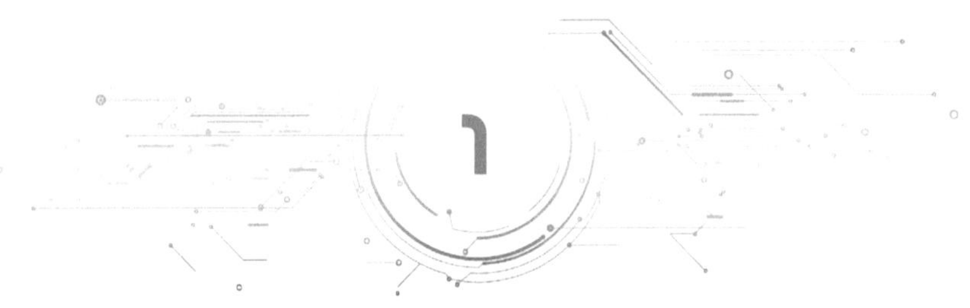

CIRCA SOONER THAN YOU THINK

Trey Primeson stood still, hesitating at the entrance to his greenhouse lest his thoughts explode and break the glass walls. Usually, he enjoyed fussing with the greenhouse controls—more light here, less water there, programming and tweaking—despite what the service recommended.

"An extra tomato every two months isn't worth the hassle," they would tell him.

But Trey knew gardening, he knew what plants needed, and he loved to put his skills to use. He remembered a time when vegetables and fruit were still flown or sailed to stores from halfway across the world. Now, growing most of your own produce was as simple as generating electricity with home solar. It was so fresh; just handling it made your hands fragrant. The refrigerator's produce compartment even sensed nutrient levels, size, and ripeness, then fed the data back to the greenhouse.

He went mindlessly back into the kitchen. Soon the doorbell rang, and an image appeared on Trey's phone screen.

The pet groomer. After a couple of minutes, he heard the door unlock and the groomer enter: Val must have swiped him in from her phone. Yes. He could hear her voice on the groomer's phone in the other room.

"So," she said, her voice thin over the speaker, "did he show the other cats their place or what? Misha's got more spunk than a teenager on steroids."

"I'm sure he does," the groomer said. A teenage kid himself, he really didn't care. Trey watched him idly on the screen from the kitchen. "Unfortunately, we had to sedate him; he's still a bit groggy. Did you want me to set the next visit on his tag?"

"Sure, I should be home soon," Val said. Where was Val? For the life of him, Trey couldn't remember. "Leave him someplace safe. Also, turn off the pet door; we don't want him going out anytime soon. Thank you so much."

The groomer reached into the carrier for Misha, a floppy, flame-point Himalayan that could easily be mistaken for a rug. He programmed the tag on the cat's bracelet for the next visit, with reminders for himself and the Primesons, and left. The door locked behind him.

After several minutes, Misha walked into the kitchen, a little unsteadily, and over to Trey, rubbing against his legs.

Trey had videoed in for his yearly physical early that afternoon with Dr. Jawar, who had known him and his family for many years. Instead of joking and asking about the family as usual, Dr. Jawar had excused himself from the chat several times to "converse" with a medical robot, asking for images, zooming in, and taking measurements. He even ordered some quick lab tests to be done. He then hopped out of the room to talk to his staff and consult with someone.

"Liver cancer" had been the words Trey heard when the doctor came back. He just sat there, refusing to believe it.

"It could be the accumulation of environmental toxins, nanoplastics, and other man-made chemicals in the liver," Dr. Jawar said. "Unfortunately, they've reached critical mass."

"But—but how could I not have a clue?" Trey said. "Sure, I've been a little tired, but I've been exceptionally busy. I feel fine otherwise. I've been sleeping very well, too. There must be some mistake."

"I'm sorry. We checked several times and my colleagues agree. The onset can be very sudden. You could've been ignoring some symptoms, attributing them to age."

The best treatment option available at this stage was a liver transplant, he said, either from a donor or with a synthetic organ. "I definitely want to see you in person here. Expect a call to schedule an appointment within a half hour." The chat had ended, and the screen went blank.

Trey looked out of the window. Then he remembered: the award ceremony!

Any other day, Trey would've walked most of the way, using moving walkways where available. Instead, he texted for a self-driving pod, and walked out of the house to the street to catch it. Several were on call there. He started for one, then received an audio alert on his phone with the correct pod number. Composing himself, he stepped back and found the one he had summoned. Too agitated to sit, he stood in the pod on the way.

"The hell!" he shouted after a few minutes while gripping the top of a seat tightly. The pod responded by displaying a series of numbers to reach out to in case of an emergency. This was no good. He messaged the pod to stop at the next intersection. He would walk the rest of the way on the busy streets, like everybody else, like everyone with a future.

History was repeating itself. But it couldn't be. More than anything, he'd wanted to not follow his dad. He remembered winning that first football game in little league. Where was Dad? He remembered getting his driver's license. Dad found out a week later. His father had had tremendous success as a professional athlete and in his careers afterward, but just before he passed away, he told Trey how much he regretted spending so much time away from his home and family. Trey had told himself that if he had a family, he'd always be there for them. "Liver cancer," the doctor had said.

Suddenly none of the streets looked like Manhattan. He checked the venue for Arianne's award ceremony. Hell, he'd entered the wrong street name. He'd ended up on the other side of the city.

His phone flashed revised directions: **This route will involve two pods and three moving walkways. You will arrive in thirty-four minutes. Would you like to summon a pod?**

No! he replied. It was too late. "Why can't these be scheduled later in the day?" he muttered to himself, turning to make his way back.

"She embodies the most effective confluence of innovation, technology, and creativity," Dr. Yang said, smiling out at the conference audience from the podium. "It's my pleasure to announce this year's Young Technologist Award winner, Arianne Primeson! May this be just the beginning of a tremendously successful career!"

Arianne stepped on the stage to applause from the people in the auditorium and the many virtual attendees, and took the plaque from Yang. The dignitaries on stage crowded around her. Slightly nervous about all the attention, she shook a few hands, trying to seem firm and confident.

"Congratulations!"

"We foresee a use for your algorithm in one of our products."

"We'll be in touch."

"Thank you, thank you," she replied. "I look forward to it." Beaming, she got offstage, descended the steps to the auditorium, and made her way to her mom, who was watching proudly.

"Oh, Arianne, what an honor, honey!" Val said as her daughter reached down to hug her. Val couldn't help noticing how much Arianne looked like her—despite being taller and bigger—with the same olive skin, dark brown hair, and delicate features.

"What's the use, though?" Arianne said, shrugging a little.

"Don't say that. You'll find projects. Bet they'll come to you now, more than you have time for."

"We'll see." Arianne smiled. "Where's Dad?" she asked, looking around.

Val's eyes darted up to the entrance one more time, searching for her husband. "Let me try again." She reached for her phone. "Trey? Trey? Hmm—not answering. Was hoping he would make it. He was definitely planning to be here."

A message appeared on her phone with Trey's location.

"Still on his way," Val said.

"Hope he at least caught the livestream," Arianne said, still in the moment and a little overwhelmed.

They made it back home several hours later. Taking a few steps into the foyer, Val saw Trey's silhouette by the window.

"Trey!" She laughed. "You scared the crap out of me. Where were you? Did you catch the award ceremony online? Innovators from top companies were there. It was amazing! Arianne was amazing! I think someone offered her a job or two."

Trey still didn't say anything.

"Were you held up with work?" Val said. She went around the house, getting work off her mind but mostly still excited about Arianne's award. "Ton of things going on this week. Chase has his baseball game on Friday, dinner with your cousin Thursday, Arianne's singing at the opening ceremony at the festival." She rambled on, letting her hair down—soft, dark brown waves cascading below her shoulders. She entered the kitchen and began putting stuff away.

"Dr. Jawar said I don't have much time left," he said after a moment.

"Time left for what?" Val said, peering into the refrigerator.

"He said the cancer is pretty late stage; a transplant is my best option."

Cancer? She froze, then turned around.

Trey explained everything. "Half his staff came by to talk to me this afternoon. Some of them asked about you."

"When—did they say when this started?" She walked over to him and put her arm around his shoulder. "How—no symptoms until now?" Tears started rolling down her cheeks. Trey shook his head, eyes getting redder, face flushed.

"Apparently that's the problem with being healthy," he said, trying to laugh. "I missed the symptoms. They said I had the vitals of someone a decade younger. They were just trying to be positive."

"Surely there're options. What about a synthetic organ? Something's got to work. As young as you are—"

"Stop being stupidly optimistic," barked Trey. Funny, that was the very trait he always found most attractive about her.

For hours they kept rehashing what he'd heard and analyzing it from various angles. The setting sun out the kitchen window turned a layer of clouds low on the horizon a deep purple.

"Arianne and Chase, what will we tell them?" Val said.

"Chase is so young," Trey said. They quietly mulled over the questions together. What if the transplant gets rejected? Could he then opt for and wait for a human donor? Considering the extent of the disease, would that leave him with even less time? They decided that some form of treatment would need to begin as soon as possible, planning for the transplant with a synthetic organ.

They told the kids after dinner that night.

"*What?* Is he going to die?" shouted Chase, his face reddening. Val could see tears welling up behind his long eyelashes.

"Mom! Why didn't you tell me right away? The award isn't more important!" Arianne cried.

Trey went over the facts with them and told them what the doctor had said. Treatment was beginning the following week. He was being referred to a world-renowned oncologist.

"Your father will get through this," Val said. "There's no reason for all of us to suspend our lives."

"Yes, Arianne," Trey said. "Make sure you visit often. Chase needs someone to wrestle him down, cut him to size!" He winked and poked Chase in his ribs.

"Daaaad!" Chase responded, fighting him off, almost laughing despite himself.

The following morning, just before heading back to work, Arianne cornered Val. "Are you going to be okay?" she said. "Wish I lived closer."

"Oh, don't worry," Val replied. "Everything will be fine. We know many people who have gone through this. Pretty routine now. Although it'd be wonderful to see you more often." She gave a quick look at the time on a laptop screen. "But, jeez, you better hurry. Aren't you late?"

"Yeah, it'll take me a half hour just to get out of the city," Arianne said, "even on those high-speed pods. I'll have to go directly to work—can't stop by the apartment."

"I need to find a project right here," Arianne said to herself as she walked out the front door.

Once aboard the unusually packed pod, she sat staring out of the window into the distance as the streets and buildings on the outskirts of the city flew by. She had planned on getting some work done during the one-and-a-half-hour ride, but she couldn't focus on anything.

Preparation for the transplant went well for Trey during the first week. His energy was returning, and most importantly he felt cheerful once again. Val decided to accompany him for one of the in-person visits.

"Let's schedule the operation for Friday next week," said Dr. Jawar.

"Sounds good. A brand-new liver then," said Trey.

"Yes, but just in case—*just in case*—it's good to establish a relationship with a grief counselor. I'd like both of you to talk to one before we operate."

"Grief counselor?" Val said. "What do you mean? Isn't the success rate one hundred percent?"

"Not exactly," said Dr. Jawar. "There are no guarantees, I'm afraid."

"Shouldn't we wait for that until I actually croak?" Trey said with a short laugh.

"Think of it as insurance," Dr. Jawar said. "I'd like to just get you on their calendar. At the very least, you can tell them some of your terrible jokes. Trust me. They can do with some of those." He winked.

Val and Trey exchanged glances.

"I'll ask them to contact you, if that's okay," Dr. Jawar said.

"Sure," said Trey.

"A Brighter Journey," the brochure read. "Where you're offered brighter options."

"What sort of hocus-pocus is this?" Trey whispered to Val as they waited for the grief counselor in Dr. Jawar's office.

The door opened, and a young woman dressed in gray walked in. "I'm Maya Okoro, from A Brighter Journey," she said.

"Wait a moment, you aren't paying my doctor under the table for this referral, are you?" Trey joked.

"What will it take to grease his palm?" said Maya, leaning over with a serious face. Then she smiled, following up with a big laugh. "No, just kidding. Our methods are also for making the stress of treatments as tolerable as possible for the whole family, so you can continue to live normal lives."

She went over virtual reality products for families, dealing with the shock, what to expect, and, of course, grief therapy sessions if necessary.

It all sounded very straightforward. "You look so healthy," Maya said. "I'm sure it won't come to that."

But it did come to that. A couple of days after the transplant, Trey went in for a checkup, expecting a complete recovery.

"I'm so sorry, Trey," Dr. Jawar said, his face solemn. "We see this happen in some cases. Your body is not accepting the synthetic liver."

"So is there anything else we can do?" asked Trey.

"We'll definitely look for a donor, but we have to monitor to see if the cancer has already started metastasizing to other organs." It all sounded so clinical and matter-of-fact. "We'll continue to keep you on the treatment for arresting metastasis."

Trey sat slumped in the self-driving pod on the way home. He called Val.

"Is everything okay?" she asked.

"The blood work didn't come out well," he said, watching the streets go by outside the pod window. "Apparently my body is rejecting the synthetic organ."

"Where are you? I should've gone with you for the appointment. Why didn't you tell me you were going?"

"Everything seemed to be going well. I didn't want to bother you. You've been working so late this week."

There was a brief pause while Val was distracted by a coworker. "Sorry, I didn't realize you were on the phone," Trey heard them saying. "No problem," Val replied. "I'll come by or call you."

Then she was talking to him again. "Trey! I would've made the time." He didn't say anything. "Trey? You there?"

"Yeah, but not sure for how long," he said, then sighed.

"What do you mean? What did Dr. Jawar say? Are you still in the clinic? Can I talk to him?"

"No. I'm on my way home. There's the option of a human donor, but the cancer shouldn't spread to other organs in the meantime."

"What did he say the chances were? Dr. Jawar will find a way. Trey!"

He didn't say anything, listening to her breathe over the phone.

"I'm coming home right now," she said. "See you in a bit."

All that Trey noticed on the way home were the everyday, mundane things—people picking up packages that delivery pods had dropped off, people walking on the busy streets as they got back to work after lunch, and an EMS pod rushing to a tall apartment building.

After he got home, Trey headed straight to the greenhouse for refuge and distraction. Their cat, Misha, followed him and sniffed a few leaves. Trey bent down and stroked his soft fur. He was still in the greenhouse with the cat when Val arrived. She walked in and hugged him tight.

"I just called Maya back; she'd been trying to reach us for a while," said Val after they'd stood in silence for several minutes, holding one another.

"Maya?" he asked.

"The counselor. We met her briefly at Dr. Jawar's office, remember?"

"Shouldn't we wait for a donor?"

Val read his face. "Gosh, no, no! She has no idea about where you are with the transplants. She said she had something else she wanted to talk to us about."

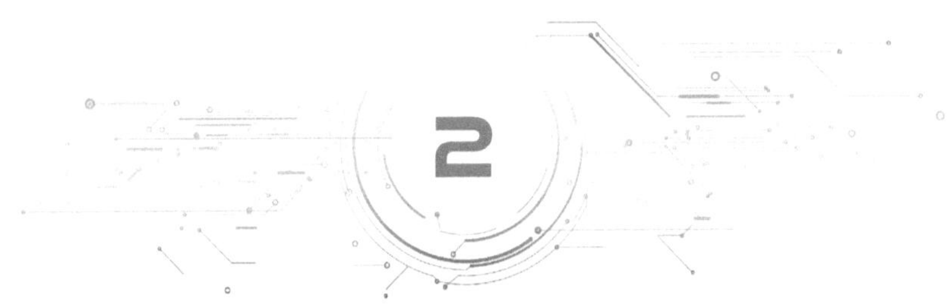

2

Arianne arrived early one evening the following week. The whole family gathered for Maya's visit.

"Hello, please come in," Arianne said, opening the door. Maya wasn't alone. Dressed mostly in gray, like Maya, was a trim young man smiling as he glanced at Maya.

"Nice to see you again," Maya said to Trey and Val. "This is my colleague Finn Karlsen." Finn flashed a very friendly smile. "Hello, young man," she said, turning to Chase. Her long black braids cascaded down as she bent to shake Chase's hand. After very brief pleasantries, Maya looked around and pointed to a cozy corner right by a large window, Misha's favorite spot. "Could we gather over there?"

"Sure," said Trey. He and Val sat on the breakfast bench.

"I can project on that wall," Maya said, waving her hand. Chase snuggled up to his mom's side. Arianne quickly adjusted the tint on the windows and sat on the window seat.

"What we're about to explain will seem like fiction," Maya said as she moved clear of the presentation on the wall. "A Brighter Journey is an offshoot of a company that makes parts for robots," she said as they all watched images and video clips of families communicating with each other with various devices. "After a decade of development and testing, we had success rates upward of eighty percent over the past couple of years. But the complexity of the technology made for slow progress. Since every person alive will eventually die, eighty percent sounded pretty good. We had our first customers over two years ago. Interest is definitely growing and ABJ, as we call it, plans on expanding operations. We're still too small for wide marketing and the resulting onslaught of customers, so we initiate all recruitment."

Val and Trey exchanged glances. Arianne leaned forward and propped her chin on her hand. Chase's eyes lit up. "Is this converting people to robots—cyborgs? Can I become a cyborg?"

"Ha! Smart boy! Not exactly," Maya said, turning to Chase with a nod and a smile. Arianne and Val gave a short laugh.

"As we were saying, it's best for families to not publicize the matter yet," Finn quickly added.

"I'm not sure we understand what you're proposing here," Trey said, unable to hold it in any longer.

Maya took a moment as she stared down at the floor, then deliberately shifted her gaze to Trey. "Essentially, we're offering eternal life," she said.

"What?" Arianne gasped. Trey leaned forward a little.

"We've developed the technology to isolate and maintain a fully functioning brain implanted with neuralware for digital input and output," Maya said. "Craniospheres or, as we affectionately call them, brain-bubbles or BBs. We'll describe neuralware in a little bit." She looked at Finn. "Normally, the body and all the organs deteriorate with time. But here, the brain lives on, with help from our neuralware."

"For how long?" Arianne asked.

"Technically . . . forever!" Finn said.

The Primesons collectively dropped their jaws, staring at Finn's symmetric face, his blond hair reflecting the light through the window.

"Is this for real?" Val asked.

"Sounds like a preview for a sci-fi movie," Trey said, turning to Val. He caught Arianne looking at him from behind.

"What—"Arianne began to ask.

At the same time, Trey started to ask, "How—"

"Please let us take you through all the information and material here before we jump into questions," Maya interrupted. "Let me say we completely understand the shock. That's the first impression most of our customers have." She smiled reassuringly.

"This isn't an elaborate gimmick, either," Finn said.

"I'll try to summarize the underlying science and engineering in simple terms," Maya said. "Neuralware is a meld of neurons and bioelectronic components organically grown and customized to fit each individual. It's been used successfully for a few years to fix neurological disorders and for implants to augment the brain's capabilities. But at ABJ, we have two specific functions for neuralware implanted in the brain: First, the embedded neurons form connections with the brain's neural network. Second, the bioelectronic components have ports to connect to and communicate with external conventional hardware, such as computers. This makes for seamless communication between the brain, in its conscious entirety, and the computer. Digital information fed to an input port is sensed directly by the brain and understood just like how we might read a web page. Speech and actions from the brain are fed through an output port to specialized auxiliary components that convert to audio and visual signals."

"So, you can talk to these…bubbles?" Arianne said, her mind racing.

"BBs for short. Yes," Maya said, pausing to catch her breath. "So the BB is maintained by ABJ—it's physically kept in our facility. If someone in your family becomes a BB, we provide you with a portal to have a 3D video chat with your BB. The video you see of the BB is an image of your choosing, usually a portrait bust of the person. You can interact with them just like you would in a 3D video chat with a normal living person. Apart from the portal, the BB can use any media to digitally communicate with anybody in the real world. They can call their friends or watch a basketball game. We also offer BBs a rich and fulfilling life in the virtual world." She paused again and looked at them. "Not what you expected to hear from a 'grief counselor,' was it?" Maya smiled.

The Primesons sat mesmerized and motionless. The projection on the wall showed a picture of a family talking to a hologram of a person. The only other light in the room other than from the projection came dimly from the window, which silhouetted Arianne in Misha's favorite spot. The cat, having weighed the option of going out through the cat door, settled with stretching out by the entryway to the kitchen.

"This is a lot of information. You have to see it for it to fully make sense," Finn said.

Trey sat with his hands clasped, fingers interlaced. Val put her hand on her husband's knee.

"I have so many questions; I don't know where to begin!" Trey said.

"Of course, of course," said Maya, nodding her head. She looked to Finn. Finn started projecting a few images and videos.

"Here're some pictures of what the 'conversion' looks like," he said. "At a very high level."

He continued while pointing at the pictures. "This person is being prepped for surgery. Here the surgeons are implanting neuralware that acts as the sole interface for all communication."

The picture showed surgeons handling several small, Jell-O-like, flexible, flesh-colored rectangular strips. A couple of strips were already implanted through the person's skull.

"It takes several weeks for the brain to accept and fuse with the implant. You can see him being monitored here. The data is being used to build the bubble. The bubble holds a suspension with nutrients that the brain needs and maintains the optimal chemistry required. Once the neuralware fuses successfully with the brain, and our team is able to send and receive signals, the brain is installed in the bubble. We use the brain's vasculature to pump in the nutrient-filled blood substitute. And for the best part," he pointed at another picture, "the family talking to their BB for the first time through the portal."

"You're able to supply the right nutrients to keep the whole brain intact and alive?" Arianne asked.

"It's the most complex and sophisticated part of the body, so it works best when we leave it mostly intact. Our blood substitute supplies a precise cocktail of nutrients essential for brain function," Finn said. "You'll see why I say 'mostly' later."

"What about aging of brain cells?" Arianne asked.

"That is precisely why I said 'mostly,'" Finn said with a smile. "If there is a region that is atrophying or is damaged, we send in nanobots to repair the cells. That's still at a very small scale. But there is a lot of cleaning that happens during the sleep cycle of the BB. We use enzymes to target and remove byproducts of metabolism that are involved in aging. It's not a perfect system. But we have seen evidence that the sleep cycle itself has extended the lifespan of these cells by a magnitude of three."

"How much testing has gone into this?" Val asked. "You talked about your success rate. Is that for real customers in just the last two years?"

"We did extensive testing before we took our first customer, so you could say about a decade," Finn said. "Also, since we develop custom neuralware and components for each BB, testing is done on the very implant that goes into each BB before the conversion."

Trey's mind was lost in thinking about the vasculature of the brain and sleep cycles.

"So you don't preserve the body, do you?" Arianne asked suddenly while glancing at her parents to see if they realized it.

Suddenly Trey's eyes got wider. It hit him. He hadn't thought of his body as a separate entity. He shifted his gaze between Maya and Finn.

"Not with our current technology," Finn said, turning to Arianne. "The brain is separated from the body before we suspend it in the bubble." Trey felt his head reel.

Arianne continued asking questions about ABJ's neuralware: whether it was built on already available modules, precisely how they slowed down the aging of brain cells, and so on.

"Sounds like you're familiar with our technology," Maya said. "You should talk to one of our engineers. I'd be happy to introduce you." She turned to Trey. "It's best to come by our labs and see all this in action," she said. "Fortunately, you're not the first ones to go through the conversion. We can schedule it for when you can meet a family going through this. Until then, don't let your mind run ragged with concern. After you visit, you might decide it's not for you. And that's fine." Trey just nodded. He was waiting to be alone.

Finn picked up the devices they had brought and then helped Arianne put the furniture they had rearranged back in order. The salesman in him came forth as he shook Trey's hand.

"We've had dozens of BBs so far," he said. "Your vitals look great, exactly what we look for in a perfect candidate. Please don't wait to make the decision until you exhaust all other options. It is important to make the conversion to a brain-bubble while you're still in good health."

It's as though he is offering a great deal on a refrigerator, Trey thought.

"Are there other people considering this right now?" Val asked. "Sort of in our stage?"

"I'm sure there are," Finn said. "Fiona?" he said, looking at Maya.

"Uh . . . yeah," Maya said.

"Would it be possible for us to chat with them? If they're interested, too, that is," Val said.

"I'll definitely find out." Maya smiled and extended her hand.

"Thanks for coming," said Val to Finn and Maya.

"Yes, yes, thank you for making the time," said Trey, his eyes focused far away.

"We'll call you with a time for the visit very soon," Maya said. "And also about Fiona."

"Visit?" Trey said.

"For you to come to ABJ for a show-and-tell," Finn said.

"Right, right," Trey said.

"Take care!" said Finn as they left.

"Conversion," Trey said aloud, raising his eyebrows as he looked around the room at the rest of the family.

"That's so cool, Dad!" Chase said.

"It's getting kind of late," Val said to Chase. "Did you shower yet?"

"Yeah, I call these my pajamas," Chase said, pulling on both pant legs.

"Get ready for bed," Val said, bending and pecking him on his cheek.

"I don't know how much of this is solidly tested. There're implants for augmenting intelligence, but this is quite extreme. What happens to the twenty-five percent that don't go through the conversion successfully?" said Arianne.

"Sounds insane," Val said. "You really don't have to do this. There are at least two other treatment options you haven't considered." Her eyes were pleading.

Trey's face relaxed. "So I'm not the only one to find this extreme," he said.

Val rubbed her husband's back as they all walked upstairs to their bedrooms.

Outside, Maya and Finn got to talking after they left the Primesons'.

"That went well," Maya said. "Thanks for coming; helps to have an engineer with me."

"Helps for me to put a face to the brain." Finn smiled. "I brought up Fiona just to . . . thought Val was looking for some reassurance."

"No worries. For sure. But Trey meeting Fiona can go either way. Could psych each other up or feed off the other's fear."

"You think he'll do it?" Finn said.

"It'll take a while for them to decide. They need to come visit. Seeing the room full of BBs has a certain effect. In there, you can tell within the first few minutes if they want to do it."

They soon came up to a moving walkway. Finn jumped on with Maya right behind.

"On to Fiona tomorrow," Maya said. "Unlike in Trey's case, there's no looming diagnosis. Convincing her will be tough. You ready?"

"Absolutely." Finn nodded. They got off another walkway.

"See you tomorrow," Maya said as she got into a pod.

"G'night!" Finn said, crossing the street.

3

Sitting in a conference room the next day, Maya flipped through Fiona's profile. Fiona had chased after skiing medals for much of her childhood and youth, then become immersed in the business of art and had been in Manhattan ever since, where she was a regular at auctions. She opened a gallery in Chelsea as uppity as the best of them out there—an international collection of artwork, a VR-fitted gallery, pretentious wine and cheese, the works. In its grand foyer was a fusion of Renaissance artwork, modern technology, and nature. Maya was lost in the VR version of the gallery.

"Sorry I'm late. Was finishing up something," Finn said, breezing into the room.

"Ahh!" Maya said. "You startled me. This is so fascinating. Look at this. What an interesting character."

"Fiona?" Finn said as he quickly skimmed some of the screens Maya pulled up.

"What's here?" Finn said, touching an icon.

It was a video of an interview in the news that featured Fiona's art gallery as one of the hottest spots in the Manhattan art scene. "I bought it in a moment of impulse about forty years ago, but I enjoyed the work so much. You have to adapt. Modern does not mean cold and sterile."

The interviewer and Fiona went back and forth for a while about the evolution of art galleries over the decades, the pre-modern era with static art, how technology had made visual arts a more vitalizing and personal experience, and so on. With the build of an Olympic athlete, Fiona looked years younger than her actual age, which was in the sixties.

Finn hit pause on the interview and turned to Maya. "Wow. I didn't know there was so much to the business of art."

"Well, it's great that she keeps up with technology," Maya said. "Makes our job a little easier."

"Seems friendly, too."

"Yeah, I bet Trey would love to talk to her about those exotic plants in the gallery."

They continued to watch the interview. When asked about her skiing accident and recovery, Fiona went on to explain that thanks to bionic prostheses, except for deep-sea diving and a few other outdoor activities, she pretty much got her life back. "Lost both my legs. Can't deny, it was devastating. Since I live by myself, I had to get used to the prostheses in a hurry. It was tough. But thanks to physical therapy—you know, where the robots are helping you move?—I was climbing stairs in no time and setting up sculptures in the gallery in just a few weeks."

Maya watched the interview and looked up events at Fiona's gallery. One was scheduled later that week, a fundraiser.

Festooned for a fundraising event, the gallery was quite stunning. Maya scanned the crowds, looking for Fiona.

"Don't you feel like we're vultures here?" she said.

"Well, that's what we do best," Finn said, looking up at a huge tree in the middle of the floor. "It's going to be a challenge convincing her to give up all of this."

Finn was looking around the grand foyer. Right next to artwork from the Renaissance era was what looked like a time portal. Some of the modern digital art dynamically incorporated visitors, standing directly in front, into their exhibits. There was another section where visitors had a full virtual-reality experience of being part of the depicted fantasy world.

It was hard to miss Fiona. Like a glass sculpture, her dewy dark skin contrasted against the silver and lacy spring-green of her jumpsuit. All she had by way of jewelry was an armlet on her left arm. With short curly hair and a regal posture, she seemed almost intimidating.

Smiling and making small talk as she went, Maya slowly made her way through a few groups of people toward Fiona. She passed a young woman who was leaning in close to a painting of a ballet dancer. She jumped away and almost bumped into Maya.

"Looks pretty real, doesn't it?" Maya smiled and nodded at the 3D projection of the ballet dancer.

"I'm so sorry. Hope I didn't step on your foot," the woman said, laughing.

"Quick, before she gets mobbed by the next group," Maya whispered to Finn, tracking Fiona from halfway across the room.

Seeing an opening in the crowd, Finn darted forward. "I am Finn, this is my partner Maya."

After a bit of small talk, Maya got straight to the point. "We have an otherworldly proposition for you. You might know our parent company—they make specialized robots."

"I already have a companion bot at home. Yeah, 'Jeeves.' Ha! That's what I call him. He's terrific. He's a butler, house-keeper, cook, and more. So I guess I'm not in the market for a companion bot," Fiona said, smiling politely.

"That's great. But our proposal is quite different," Maya said.

"What do you see yourself doing in five years? How about something more real than that?" Finn asked, pointing to the fantasy VR world he and Maya had just walked by. "What if you could dynamically curate your entire reality? Forever."

"You call that real?" Fiona said, tilting her head toward Finn.

Finn gave a sheepish grin.

"But tell me more. Is this a practical joke?" Fiona said with a smile.

"Have you heard of neuralware or augmented intelligence? If you have some time, we'd love to show you," Finn said.

"I bet you haven't seen anything like this before," said Maya.

"Okay?" Fiona looked from Maya to Finn. "Is this something I can use in the gallery? I'm always looking for new technology."

"Oh, I don't see why not," Maya said, then turned to Finn. "Right?"

"Sure," Finn said. "We aren't the creative types, but I bet you can."

"Send me some samples," Fiona said. "Video? If anybody has used it for art, I'd love to see."

"Great!" Finn said. "But I am afraid it's proprietary, and I can't share video yet."

"We'll keep it very brief," Maya said. "And we're not too far away. Do you have any time next week?"

Fiona spoke into her armlet, which evidently was connected to her computer. After a few seconds, she said, "How about Thursday? Early afternoon?"

Maya created an event in her calendar. Then she connected Fiona's and Finn's phones to the event. The event popped up on Finn's phone, and he added ABJ's address.

"Enjoy the tour," said Fiona with a sweep of her arm. "You have to immerse yourself to get the whole experience."

"We indeed have," Maya said.

"It's spectacular!" Finn said and then pointed to the middle of the foyer. "With all the technology around, that tree is my favorite."

"Well, we're looking forward to seeing you Thursday," Maya said.

"Likewise," Fiona said.

Maya and Finn briskly made their exit.

4

ater that week, Fiona stood deep in thought in front of a new exhibit that was still in pieces. Her walking, talking virtual office assistant announced, "Meeting with Lars, architect and director of virtual reality in five minutes." She had about an hour. Her next appointment appeared on the display: 2:00 p.m. ABJ.

She threw a glance at the entrance and spoke to her assistant, "Catch me up on what Lars has been up to the last two years."

The assistant reeled off, "Lars undertook a recent project revolutionizing tourism around an ancient temple. Buttressed walkways and Disney-style rides combined with strategically placed augmented and virtual reality experiences around the monument to control traffic and prevent the structure from collapse. While the intent was preservation, Lars centered all the publicity and marketing around personalizing the experience, state-of-the-art technology, and entertainment. After all, it wasn't practical to persuade the millions of tourists to stay away in order to save the temple from damage."

She moved one of the pieces in the exhibit away from the center and walked toward the entrance.

"Congratulations!" Fiona said. "I heard about your latest projects."

"Thank you," Lars said. "Must say, I . . . owe it all to the implant."

Fiona raised her eyebrows. "Implant?"

"You know my background," he said, "mostly engineering for virtual reality. So I went in for a neuralware implant for architectural knowledge."

"I've heard of those things. What's it like? You just wake up one day feeling like an architect?" Fiona said, laughing.

"Ha! More gradual than that," he said. "It's this bundle of neurons and hardware, I am told. As long as you can give it time to take root and establish connections up here, it works." Lars pointed to his head. "It's almost like someone else is doing all the hard work of learning and practicing while you sleep, and you wake up to the benefits."

"Really?" Fiona said. "I've gotten a lot of companies offering the latest bionic extensions and prostheses since my accident. Some want to replace my organs with synthetic ones with longer lifespans. Apparently it's easy to connect to and monitor them."

"I've heard of that," Lars said. "Many people, normal healthy people, are opting for a synthetic organ even in place of the perfectly fine functioning ones they have. But this is nothing like that. I was promised that I'd acquire architectural knowledge including the kind of in-depth analysis and inferential understanding that comes from years of study."

"Fascinating. So it works!" Fiona said.

"It was definitely worth it."

"I can see that," Fiona said, remembering Maya and Finn's proposal.

"'Doing time at university will be a thing of the past,' the neuralware company claims."

"'Doing time'? As in the years spent earning a diploma or certification? No need to spend years studying?"

"Nope," Lars replied. "Ideas connecting virtual reality and architecture just seem natural to me now. It opened up a whole new field of work for me."

"Well, congratulations again," she said. "The new exhibit is right there. Work your magic. Take your time, and let me know what your suggestions are. My assistant is here if you need anything. I have an appointment to get to."

<hr>

After bidding Lars goodbye, Fiona got to thinking on her way to A Brighter Journey. Except for the accident, she felt very fit and healthy. Her life seemed fine. But just that morning, her sister Simona was talking about plans she was making for the next stage of life with her partner. "You'll look for a big change, too, just watch it," Simona had said. "Perhaps find a partner." Fiona started wondering about the stages of life. She had considered Simona an ever-present, permanent part her life. And now it seemed like Simona could be moving away from the city. *Am I actually longing for a partner?* Fiona thought.

Fiona got off the pod and walked briskly, looking for ABJ's entrance. A comical-looking figure of a human skeleton inside a window caught her attention. She walked back to the entrance, entered the lobby, and messaged Finn.

"Welcome! How're you doing?" Finn said after she was ushered in from the lobby.

"Fiona will be here shortly. I'm her avatar," Fiona said with affected sincerity.

"All avatars need to check in with Democritus right there," Finn said, pointing to the skeleton.

"Oh?" Fiona said. "I thought it was a failed conversion." They both laughed.

"The team is excited to meet you," Finn said as he led her through a hallway into a small meeting room where Maya and a few others were ready with a detailed show-and-tell. Maya started with the usual introduction.

"Pardon me, but I just have to," Fiona interrupted. "We aren't talking replacing limbs and organs with synthetic equivalents, right?"

"Not at all," Finn said.

Maya gave the overview: Irreversible conversion. Eternal life. Many successful conversions so far.

This is even more futuristic than what I heard from Lars, Fiona thought. She was briefly reminded of what Simona said, again. Maya continued to talk about the surgery, neuralware, and communication channels with family and friends, then Finn explained the emotional aspects of the conversion. According to the team, Fiona had not much to lose but a whole lot to gain. Not only would she continue to live a full life, she could have a richer experience in the virtual realm.

"To sum it up," Finn said, "imagine if you moved to an island of your dreams and could keep in touch with your family and friends just the same, only through digital media."

Now Fiona was starting to believe that this was neither a scam nor was it too outlandish. A sandy beach. Blue waters. Even a forest thrown in, and why not? But is that what would constitute a fulfilling "next stage"? What about companionship?

"You haven't said a word," Finn said. "Hope we didn't shock you." He smiled. Fiona, seemingly deep in thought, just nodded. She shook off her visions of a gorgeous yet lonely island.

"It's quite all right not to know what to make of it all," Maya said. "It will take time for it to sink in."

"We understand you need time to process all the information," Finn said.

"Feel free to discuss it with close family and friends," Maya said. "Call us anytime you have a question or just want to talk about this."

"Most fascinating for sure," Fiona said. "I'll need to sleep on it. And as you said, I need to talk to my family, who probably won't believe me at first." She stood up to leave, extending her hand.

Maya took her hand between both of her own. "You'd make a fantastic BB, 'BBFiona,'" she said.

"I'm sure," Fiona said, smiling. It sounded like an honorific.

Back at the gallery, Fiona stood in front of the new exhibit that Lars had been helping with earlier. Forever. It sounded concrete and comforting. *I almost died after the skiing accident. Why should I ever die? What would Simona say? Would she think this is too crazy? Or would she approve of this "next stage" of life? And neuralware—not only is Lars alive and kicking, he's now a competent and wildly successful architect. Have I been limiting my scope? Could I be doing so much more with my life?*

"So what do you think?" Fiona said after relating the whole ABJ story to her sister over the phone.

"Most . . . fantastical," Simona said.

"So you think I should go ahead."

"No, I didn't say that! I'm coming over tonight. Let's talk."

"I'll have Jeeves make some pavlova."

"With rum sauce?"

"You got it."

———

"Did madam have a nice day?" Jeeves asked as soon she entered her apartment.

"Indeed, madam did," Fiona replied in the same accent.

The company that had sold her Jeeves, AmieBots, had done a great job of customizing it to Fiona's very specific physical needs. With a sturdy sawhorse-like design, Jeeves was built for lifting heavy objects. "He" also had the dexterity and motor skills to cook and do household chores. And a personality like most companion bots. For the fun of it, Fiona had initially set his accent to early twentieth-century British. She'd gotten so used to Jeeves that on occasion she inadvertently personified him, saying something tender, until a canned response brought her back to reality.

"Too bad you're not my type, Jeeves!"

"Madam can change my preferences. Let me know if you need instructions."

"You're fine. You're keeping me from needing a meaningful relationship, though."

"As you wish, madam."

Fiona peeked into the hallway. Although she could talk to him from anywhere in the apartment, she liked to see the robot when she did.

"So, Jeeves, Simona should be here in an hour."

"Would madam like me to make a pavlova?" asked Jeeves.

"Oh, Jeeves, you read my mind. Make sure we have rum sauce."

"Certainly, madam," Jeeves said, then went into the kitchen.

At Fiona's request, Jeeves had already helped gather information about A Brighter Journey, including a news article about PanGalaxias's upcoming project, that had a short reference to a collaboration with ABJ. Fiona followed the obscure link about the collaboration. PanGal was widely known for space exploration and travel. They had received authorization to plant organisms found to thrive in extreme environments, such as the Antarctic, on Jupiter's moon Europa. "Observing how the bacteria establish themselves and evolve would be tremendously informative for evolutionary biologists and scientists trying to find the origin of life and astrobiologists searching for extraterrestrial life," the article said. *Pretty cool,* she thought.

Simona arrived on time, as usual. Jeeves verified her image in the camera above the front door, unlocked it, and informed Fiona of her arrival.

Simona had barely stepped through the door before she began talking. "You didn't sign up already, did you?" she said. "Would be just like you to do it before telling anyone. Like the time you volunteered to fix research stations on the far side of the moon."

"Oh no! I wouldn't do it," Fiona said. "It's irreversible."

Simona took her shoes off, perched on the sofa, and rummaged through some chocolates on a side table.

"Guess what Jeeves made?" Fiona said, pointing to the kitchen counter.

"Oh, Jeeves!" Simona said. "My favorite dessert. I need to get me a Jeeves."

"You called, madam?" Jeeves said. "If you're looking for a companion bot, contact AmieBots. I could set up a visit if you'd like. They're twenty minutes from here."

"Perhaps later, Jeeves," Simona said.

"So . . . ," Fiona said. Then she went over the details about ABJ and the conversion. Simona had already done some research and read about similar tech; she finished some of Fiona's sentences.

"Funny news, madams," Jeeves said softly.

"Yes, Jeeves?" Simona said. "I'm all ears."

"Innerings, the space junk removal company, threatens Weihua," Jeeves said. "Pay up by the month's end for the removal or we'll land your space junk on your property."

"And your response to that?" Fiona ribbed her sister.

"How does he find these things?" Simona said and smiled. "But back to you. For the record, I'm still on the fence," Simona said. "But I found something about ABJ that'll blow your socks off."

"Is it about PanGal? Yeah, Jeeves pulled it up for me."

"I should've guessed," Simona said.

"Isn't that just too enticing? I forgot to ask Maya about it."

"Right. But I wonder. That's from sometime back; there's nothing else about it since. It's all about ABJ's creative programs for grief management. Are they telling you everything?"

"I have a call with them soon. I'll find out more."

Fiona moved on to other topics. They had a good dinner and Simona bid goodbye with a "Don't rush into anything."

"I won't," Fiona said.

"Jeeves, can you connect me with Maya at ABJ?" Fiona said first thing in the morning.

"Great to hear from you," Maya said. "One moment. Let me get Finn in here, too."

"Hi, Fiona," Finn said. "Our team is excited to give you a demonstration. We were wondering about your availability. Might have to be late in the afternoon or evening. Sorry, did you have a question?"

Fiona brought up the news article about PanGal. "Where does ABJ fit in with a company that does work on other planets?"

Maya and Finn looked at each other. "Uhh, yeah . . . right," Maya said.

Finn quickly jumped in. "Yeah, so PanGal is interested in the applicability of our tech for deep-space travel—for extending the reach of space travel. They could have a whole crew on board who can run the ship on very limited resources."

"Are you saying that I could be part of PanGal?" Fiona said. "Possibly even volunteer for such an expedition if I go through with the conversion? At my age?" Fiona said.

"We're talking about your BB here, so age is hardly a factor," Maya said. "I'd imagine that the health and vitality of your BB would determine—but we are getting ahead of ourselves here. Sorry, but we simply aren't privy to such details about PanGal. Let's talk about practical matters."

After a back-and-forth about how long the conversion process took, the risks involved, and backup plans, if any, Finn looked for an opening and asked if Fiona would be interested in observing how a BB communicated and interacted with the world. "Someone's gone through the conversion recently and is ready to meet their family for the first time," he said.

"I think it's best that you see it in action," Maya said. "We'll get the family's consent so you can observe."

"I'd like that. Let me know when, and I'll clear my schedule," Fiona said.

"Don't rush the decision," Simona had said. Was she rushing?

The "idea room" at AmieBots was buzzing with activity. Chairs, made of recycled plastic in a vibrant color palette, looked like 3D jigsaw puzzle pieces. The ceiling was a maze of glass panes arranged in a deliberately haphazard way, generating the urge to straighten the creases out. The outside walls were clear glass. The inside walls served as whiteboards on which drawings of circuit diagrams and process flows could come alive in simulation. Ozzie Sargsyan, pale as the wall next to him, was sitting with a bunch of other engineers and artists waiting for Alex, their CEO. All were dressed in casual clothes, but Ozzie went further with a crumpled T-shirt and dark curly hair down to his shoulders clearly in need of a good brushing.

"You think he's going to talk about quarterly earnings?" one of the engineers asked Ozzie.

"Yeah. Don't know what else we can do," Ozzie said. "Just too many competitors. But I still say, our companion bots are way more realistic than most out there."

Alex walked in and got straight to the point. "I'm sorry," he said, his face creased with concern, "but if we don't up our game, this company is going down. Everybody and his brother is making bots these days. Have you heard the latest? Bots are now sold in packs, as 'instant families.'" He rolled his eyes.

"But we have solid neuroscience behind our products," said one of the engineers.

"So?" Alex said. "Look at the gimmicks and marketing we're up against! We need to pull away from the competition with something totally new. How about we give our bots a unique and authentic personality?"

"I wouldn't mind one myself," Ozzie said almost under his breath. "One that can land me a second date."

"Can't have worse luck than me," the guy sitting next to him said.

"Kidding me?" Ozzie whispered back to him. "I don't even ask for much. Just no games, no hoodwinking."

"Multi-dimensional, sometimes even a controversial personality," Alex continued. "That should make our competition look like soft toys in comparison!"

"How about I go pretend to be a bot?" said someone in the back of the room.

"Any other ideas?" Alex said. Several others chimed in with suggestions.

"How come nobody's using cloning?"

"You mean create the customer's clone?"

"Who'd be in charge?"

"Could we use gene editing to make the clone smarter?"

"Roles would get reversed, wouldn't they? You'd be your clone's slave then."

The conversation steered toward imprisoning the clone— making sure the original was in control. Wasn't there an old sci-fi movie on that theme? But how would they comply with the code of ethics? The group went on brainstorming wildly for a while. Alex encouraged everyone to think of innovative ideas, then he ended the meeting.

Ozzie left the idea room when he ran into a woman he had been meaning to introduce himself to.

"Are you new here at AmieBots?" he said, mustering enough courage to strike up a conversation.

"Priya," she said. She seemed to recognize him. "Aren't you… Ozzie?"

He couldn't remember if they had ever met.

"Yeah, saw you at the . . . meeting the other day," he said awkwardly. "Working late?"

Ozzie's intentions were clear from his body language, and Priya responded favorably. More pleasantries followed. Ozzie proposed to "get to know her better" in many indirect ways. She repeatedly kept bringing the conversation back to work opportunities for her in Ozzie's group. She tried to end the conversation and leave, but Ozzie kept talking until he saw a man pop into the lobby and wave to her.

"I gotta go," he said. He turned around and walked away, swearing under his breath. "They're all the same."

At home, Ozzie started surfing the freeNet endlessly. Clues for the big idea were out there somewhere, he knew. Companion robots were being sold in all sizes and species, including the garden variety that fetched you food and drink and flattered you whenever possible. Maybe somebody had already created a wife bot—to hell with all the awkwardness of meeting and dating. To hell with rejections. At two in the morning, every web page he ran into was filled with advertisements for digital immortality: someone in the tech world was making money off faking the continued existence of a loved one after death—another flavor of the VR personality simulator that psychologists and counselors had been using, perhaps.

Low-level AI will do, thought Ozzie. *Just learn the dead person's social persona and interactions over the years to continue mimicking their messaging.*

But Alex had challenged them to find ideas for a realistic bot; one that was not only convincing in the digital world but was as unique and unpredictable as a real person, complete with the flaws, irrationalities, and insecurities that make a human being genuine. About to turn in for the night, he ran into a news item about A Brighter Journey. Although short on detail, the article piqued his interest.

If I don't make it in life by forty, I want my brain in a bubble. And to what end, he thought.

"Holy shit!"

In a frenzy, Ozzie started fleshing out the thought. It seemed too good to work. He jumped up and started drawing and designing on a small digital whiteboard. He considered calling Alex, but it was still dark out.

Soon the sun rose bright but benevolent, which he hardly noticed after the all-nighter. He rushed to work, where he grabbed Alex and pulled him into a small meeting room.

"I've got it! I've got it! You have to listen to this."

"Another of your crazy ideas?" Alex said. "Shortest elevator pitch please; I have an appointment in ten minutes."

6

"**A**ren't you going into the office today?" Val asked as she was headed out the door.

"No. Have to figure this out first," Trey said, picking his head up from trying to debug the electronic circuitry that wasn't working. "I promised the team I'd have it for the satellite launch this week."

"Good. Chase needs you for something later in the afternoon."

"K." After a while he huffed and threw himself back in the chair. He stared out of the window. Then he got up and made his way into the greenhouse. Misha followed him in, chasing and batting a small wool ball. Trey picked the cat up and stroked his back. After a couple of seconds, Misha wriggled out of his arms and bounded back into the kitchen. Trey heard a call coming in.

"Hello? Trey?"

"Yes?" Trey said without paying much attention to who it was.

"Hey, this is Maya. How're you doing?"

"Yeah. Hi, Maya."

"Can you and Val make it to a live demonstration?" Maya said. "One of the BBs, Glen, had a successful surgery. His family is going to be here when he wakes up. They said you can come and observe. Sorry this is such short notice, but it's this afternoon at three. Would that work?"

"Hmm," Trey said. "Let me ask Val."

"I can hold," Maya said.

Trey texted Val: **ABJ this afternoon at 3? Maya wants to show us something.**

Val replied: **Should be fine.**

Trey told Maya he and Val would be there.

"Okay, great! Let me know when you get here," Maya said. "I just created an event with both you and Val. You should have the address."

"Hmm . . . yes," Trey said.

Val decided to go home early in the afternoon so she and Trey could go to ABJ together. After they got off the self-driving pod, Trey walked with his gaze down, both hands in his pockets. Val held his elbow, steering him away from people and around a trash compactor.

"We're only going to observe today," Val said. "There's no need to make any decisions."

"Right," he said.

"Jeez, I didn't think it'd be this busy," Val said. "Is something going on?"

"I think they're here down the street," Trey said.

Barely distinguishable from its neighbors, A Brighter Journey looked like any other electronics and hardware outfit. Facing the street were many windows. Along the windows on the inside was seating in pleasing colors. Trey and Val entered to find a much larger workspace on the inside with ample daylight. The workspace was largely open but for a few rooms with doors. Several women and men were piecing together circuitry around all manner of automated bots. Trey texted Maya.

Maya texted back: **Please have a seat. Give me a few.**

Trey and Val sat down.

After about fifteen minutes, Finn rushed out of a door leading to an interior hallway.

"So sorry!" Finn said, fidgeting nervously. "There was a hiccup with waking BBGlen. Would it be okay if we got back to you with another day and time?"

"A hiccup?" Trey said, looking at Val with alarm.

"What's going to happen now? Can he be revived?" Val said.

"Oh, of course. We're all working on it," Finn said. "Maya is with the family now. Again, I'm sorry we dragged you down here for nothing."

Trey stood, staring in the general direction of the comical-looking skeleton at the far end of the lobby.

"I guess we should go then," Val said, touching Trey on his arm.

"This is . . . ," Finn said, "quite normal. Happens from time to time."

"Right," Trey said, turning to Finn. "We understand."

Once outside ABJ, Trey headed to the nearest moving walkway. Val hurried to keep up with him. She tried to get close enough just to say, "It's okay," but Trey kept up his speed, almost bumping into a criminal serving time fitted with special VR goggles. On the unusually crowded moving walkway, Trey hailed for a self-driving pod.

They both got into the pod and sat down. Val reached out and held his hand.

"I'm fine," Trey said, looking out of the window.

"Finn said it happens all the time," Val said. "But you really don't . . ."

"Yeah, I know. Doesn't seem reliable." Trey shook his head and sighed. "Back to therapies and transplants."

A couple of days later, Maya called Val.

"How's Trey feeling?" Maya said.

"He's coping, I guess," Val said.

"So sorry about what happened the other day, but BBGlen has come around. While it might seem alarming to you, it's not so uncommon for us. We expect things will go smoothly this time. Would you and Trey want to come by?"

"When were you thinking?" Val said. "I'd like Arianne to be there, too. Evenings would work better."

"Scheduling would depend on BBGlen's family. I'll find out more and message you."

A week later, Arianne joined Trey and Val at ABJ to watch BBGlen's awakening.

"Aren't we crazy to even consider this after what happened last time?" Val whispered to Arianne.

"Dad won't need this. He'll get a transplant. I'm here to see the cool tech," Arianne whispered back.

Maya hurriedly rushed in and out of a couple of rooms, her forehead glistening. She waved, smiling apologetically, and signaled to them to wait. Eventually Finn appeared and ushered them through a long hallway to a few empty seats in the back of a dimly lit room. After their eyes adjusted to the low light, they saw that many people were in the room waiting with silent apprehension. Several seemed to be from ABJ itself and were quietly discussing technical details. Arianne looked around. The mostly empty and sterile-looking stage up front had a partition at the back that served as a display screen, momentarily showing a bird's-eye view of beautiful land-scapes, earthly and extraterrestrial. In the middle of the stage was a light green circular pedestal, about the size of a barstool. A monitor on the right had all sorts of data scrolling on it. Her eye caught molar concentrations of various compounds, fluid pressure, and more. *Fluid pressure must be the equivalent of blood pressure*, Arianne thought. To the left was a semicircular curved screen behind which a few ABJ scientists seemed huddled around something. They talked in low voices and frequently looked up at the display monitor. Several thick white conduits ran across the stage and behind the partition.

After a few tense moments, the technical team gave the final go from behind the curved screen, and Maya's team went to the green pedestal.

"This is exactly the portal you will be using at home," Maya said, looking at the people seated in the middle of the first few rows. A projection of a keyboard appeared to one side of the pedestal. One of the team members made a few selections on the keyboard. BBGlen's bust, a 3D hologram, appeared above the pedestal.

"Just like a 3D video chat," Maya continued while looking up at the people seated in the back. "This 3D rendering uniquely identifies the person behind the BB, giving the family and the group a sense of visual connection."

"BBGlen can receive all sensory input now," Maya said, "as though he is physically right here in front of us."

People sat up and leaned forward in the room. A couple of children craned their necks around the adults in front.

Val gripped Trey's hand. She couldn't take her eyes off BBGlen.

"It's just a 3D picture of the man," Trey whispered to her. Arianne heard him and rolled her eyes at her dad. Trey winked at her, and they exchanged a quick smile.

"Glen?" Maya called. "Glen? Give us a sign if you can hear me."

"Yes. I'm here. Yes," a voice said. The 3D hologram came alive. The lips moved; the hologram looked like a live video feed! There was a collective murmur in the room.

"Either this is a well-executed illusion or some really advanced tech," Trey whispered. The room was thick with apprehension.

"Talk as you normally would," Maya said. "No need to stress yourself out."

"So I have to picture myself speaking, pretend to move my lips, and get the words out," the hologram said.

"Glen?" a gray-haired lady called out. "Is it really you?"

"It's me," he said, then called out the names of people he could recognize—about six people who sat right up front. They stood up, waving, making gestures, and congratulating him.

"Mom?" he said again.

The gray-haired lady almost collapsed. "Honestly I . . . I . . . had no faith that this was going to work," she said, then took a handkerchief out to wipe her eyes. BBGlen's image gazed at Fiona.

"Sorry for crashing your family gathering," Fiona said. "I'm Fiona. I'm considering the conversion."

The Primesons exchanged glances. They looked at Fiona—physically fit, charming, and full of life. Trey leaned over to whisper to Val but stopped as he heard BBGlen responding.

"Oh no, not a problem. Greetings from the other side, I guess," BBGlen said and chuckled. "I'm still figuring all this out. Feels like I was hit in the head, knocked unconscious, and now I'm having this out-of-body experience. It's weird."

The ABJ team gathered around the pedestal, each person going through a different sensory input and then observing and recording the response from BBGlen's hologram projection.

"Follow the pointer," said one of them as she moved around the pedestal, checking BBGlen's range of vision.

"Close your eyes and let me know when I touch your shoulder," said another. They tested every aspect of the portal and the 3D projection of Glen's face. A couple of people from

BBGlen's family gathered around to watch. The others were talking among themselves.

Trey imagined himself in Glen's place. He overheard someone say, "He can go and see whatever he wants at any moment." *How ironic*, he thought. Glen seemed trapped and reduced to a hologram. He glanced at Fiona, wondering if she thought the same.

"Let's talk to her. She doesn't seem to be agonizing over the decision," Trey whispered.

"Perhaps—" Val started to say.

"Bet this is a choice for her," Trey said.

"As it is for you," Val said, looking into Trey's eyes.

Trey looked away from Val and at the scientists on the stage, then he thought about his recent visit with Dr. Jawar.

Maya now addressed BBGlen's inner circle of family and friends, the six sitting right up front. "Let's test if messaging is working okay in your FamilyZone," she said. "That's how you'll communicate with your BB if you're not in front of the 3D portal. Use any device, just like you would for a social media group. ABJ sets up two mandatory virtual groups, called zones, for BBs to be part of. There's the FamilyZone, which is for Glen's close circle of family and friends, and the BBZone, a community exclusively for BBs. BBs present themselves as their former real-life personas and physical forms in these two zones. The BBZone is also used by ABJ for sending messages and general monitoring. Most importantly, these two zones serve as anchors or reference points linking BBs back to their former real lives."

Finn noticed that Glen's people were bombing his FamilyZone with text messages using their phones. "Give him time to respond," he said. "He's not Superman. Remember, it's just good old Glen behind all that."

BBGlen confirmed that he received their messages and responded as well.

"So let's end this call on the 3D portal. How about you make a simple audio call after?" Finn said to BBGlen.

"Yes, baby," the gray-haired lady said. "I can hear you; can you hear me?" She kept looking at the pedestal.

"It's just like a phone call," Finn said. "You can do this from anywhere; you don't need the portal."

"How're you feeling?" she said into her phone. "Are you tired?" She spoke for a little while, then asked him to rest and hung up.

Finn called BBGlen back on the 3D portal again.

"It felt like he was still alive somewhere, talking to me," the lady said to her neighbor.

"I am alive," BBGlen said from the portal, and the hologram smiled.

"There are many social media groups that BBs can create and be part of," Finn said. "Membership is at will, unlike the FamilyZone and the BBZone. The others are purely for entertainment and enrichment. BBs choose their own made-up avatars and specific personas. Essentially it's a group of avatars interacting with each other. Glen?" he said, turning to the portal. "Can you share your experiences in the Virtual Zones so far? You've had barely any time, but tell us which VZones you're part of and about your avatars."

"I'm a forest ranger in one of the VZones," BBGlen said. "I get to guide the other avatars through virtual clones of rain forests that I have actually been to. There's this other VZone for playing Jenga. There are about six of us in the zone, stacking blocks and pulling them out. So my avatar itself is a block. The other avatars were confused the first time I burst out of the stack and crashed everything." He laughed.

"The appearance of the setting, the ecosystem, and the whole milieu of a VZone are completely customizable by the BBs," Finn said. "The event horizon of a black hole could be a VZone if a BB chooses."

"I'm thinking of starting a VZone for those interested in magic," BBGlen said. He paused as the whole room thought about what he had just said. "C'mon, people. That's a joke!" He chuckled.

"That's my Glen," his mother said with a sigh. "Lived to make others laugh."

"Living, Mom. I am still here."

Maya and team continued to explain the workings of a BB and how research was underway for more tactile inputs and outputs to extend the BB experience to the physical world.

"You mean I'll be able to hug my son one day?" Glen's mom asked.

"Yes, ma'am," Finn said. "One day, in the not very distant future, you won't be able to tell the difference between a BB and a real person."

"Can we see BBGlen, you know the . . . actual BB?" asked someone seated up front.

"Would love to see the real thing," Arianne whispered to Val.

"Maybe later," Maya said. "Our team is usually busy doing maintenance there. We limit visits to a couple of people at a time." Saying that BBGlen and his family needed some private time, Maya led the Primesons and Fiona out of the room. She thanked them for coming and said she hoped that viewing BBGlen's awakening firsthand was informative and helpful. Fiona started walking toward the lobby.

"I'm Trey," he said, catching up to Fiona and extending his hand.

"Nice to meet you," Fiona said. And after a quick glance at the rest of the Primesons, she said, "I take it you're considering."

"Indeed. You, too?" Trey said.

"A step before that, if there's one," Fiona said. "I'm in no rush. Need more time to think, I guess."

"Of course," Trey said, drawing himself back a little bit. He glanced at Val, who gave him a reassuring smile.

"You look familiar," Arianne said to Fiona.

"Oh? Just one of those people," Fiona said, smiling. "I'd love to chat more. So sorry, but I have to run."

"Let's keep in touch," Val said.

"Absolutely," Fiona replied. They exchanged contact information.

Trey, Val, and Arianne stepped out of ABJ. People walked hurriedly by, zigzagging around them. Pods kept whizzing by, and so did several delivery drones overhead.

"Are you okay?" Val said. "You're walking funny."

"No, just adjusting to the light," Trey said, trying to shake himself back to reality. Nothing looked the same anymore. *This street wouldn't be real for the BBs*, he thought. *It's as though they're inhabiting a parallel universe.* He looked around at the people going about their business in the glorious sunshine. *Do the BBs miss this? Do they regret their decision?*

"I can't believe there was a real person behind that hologram. And the graphics and videography in the VZones looked spectacular," said Arianne.

"Yes, it was enticing, but life as we all know it would change," Val said. "There is that other clinical trial!"

"It's also irreversible, Dad," Arianne said.

"So is death," Trey murmured. "So is death," he said again, slowly. *Maya said you could create the life of your dreams with the people of your choice*, he thought. "Death will slowly become an archaic concept," she had said.

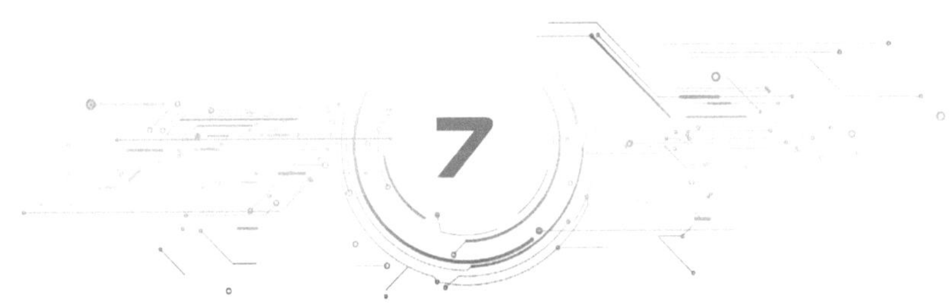

The cancer had metastasized to one of his lungs—it was clear in the images. Trey sat in the doctor's office, his eyes closed. The nurse bot checked him in, took his vitals, and finished the scans.

"Trey, it's nice to see you again," it said. "Dr. Jawar will be here in a moment. Is there anything else I can do for you?"

The bot's voice was soothing and believably caring, but Trey could only mumble. "Ummm I'm fine," he said.

After a moment, Dr. Jawar walked in and stood right by Trey, laying a hand on his shoulder with an affectionate squeeze.

"You do want to try the clinical trial, don't you?" he said. "For the improved version of a synthetic liver? I'm about to sign you up. We can use standard therapy for the cancerous lung. That is the best course of action now."

But it was risky, Trey knew, especially at this stage in the progression of the disease. What if participation in a clinical trial, which might not work, meant that conversion to a BB wasn't possible? What if it really was the end?

"Do we know how quickly the cancer is progressing?" he asked.

"It is aggressive," Dr. Jawar said, looking down. "But," he nodded and looked into Trey's eyes, "transplanting synthetic organs is becoming quite common. Really, the fairy tale of a fully bionic human is soon to become reality. But still, there will be a definite risk."

"Let me think about it."

"Absolutely, Trey. We're right here for you," Dr. Jawar said. He stood there shaking Trey's hand for a while.

That evening, Trey was in the kitchen, rummaging through the refrigerator, pulling out several bottles and tossing them on the counter. He opened a few packages of crackers, looked at the expiry date, and tossed them by the bottles. He heard Val walk into the house.

"Well, I told him I'll think about it," he called. Val came into the kitchen.

"What? What's going on?" she said, looking at the mess. Then she remembered. "Did you just see Dr. Jawar? What did he say?"

"Wanted me to sign up. I am not ready! What if I want to go the BB route?" Trey sounded angry.

"Okay," Val said.

"Okay what?" he said. "Now you don't have an opinion on this?" He couldn't help himself. He sent another bottle rolling down the counter. It rolled into the sink with a crash.

"Trey! I know this is hard. We can have all sorts of opinions, but *you* have to decide," she said. She leaned on the counter next to the refrigerator. They heard Arianne coming into the kitchen.

"Listen to this!" she said, bursting in. "There's a study that found a link between neuralware implants and feeling more ticklish." She had been following the latest research and shared the more amusing findings from time to time. Chase followed her, as he usually did.

"Tickle, tickle," he said, jumping around and trying to dig into anybody's side he could reach. Trey's face relaxed into a smile.

The following day, Trey told Maya over the phone he was "definitely considering" the conversion. Being quite familiar with how nerve-wracking the decision could be, Maya referred the Primesons to ABJ's psychologist, who spent a great deal of time over a couple of weeks answering questions and assessing their emotional preparedness.

"If you could, think of the surgery and recovery as a sabbatical," he said.

"Hardly," Trey said. "A sabbatical feels like a vacation."

"Remember, this is a choice, not exactly like an emergency procedure in a hospital. In our experience, the separation of a sabbatical frees up all parties to deal with the physical and practical demands of the conversion."

"More like an exile into the twilight zone," Trey smirked, leading to nervous smiles around the room. "I'm sorry, this is eating me up." He hung his head low, and Val put her arm around her husband's shoulder with a sigh.

"Absolutely, Trey," the psychologist said. "Not a decision to be made lightly, not for the faint of heart. Cancer does not choose. But ABJ does. The conversion is for someone who's not just physically strong but also mentally unshakable. The psychological aspect comes into play, especially after the conversion. There's no coming back. The adjustment period is tough. BBs tell us of panic attacks and sleep paralysis."

"Feels like I'd be stuck in a video game forever," Trey said with eyes focused far away.

"Will he be able to see my game?" Chase asked. "He's gonna be always online?"

"Yes, anytime you want him to," the psychologist said, patting Chase on his knee.

"So I can play online games with him, even in the middle of the night?"

"That's a question for your mother, Chase!" The psychologist smiled and turned to Trey. "On a more serious note, BBs do need rest. A shorter time than us, but they definitely need to give the brain time to perform normal maintenance."

"I could do with some sleep right now," Trey said. He couldn't remember the last time he had a good night's sleep.

Next, the Primesons met ABJ's conversion team in a conference room. They explained the process, detailing the options at each stage if something should go wrong. The whole family sat quietly, listening to the team describe the numerous junctures where things could fail.

Seeing the concern on their faces, one of the ABJ team tried to be reassuring.

"It's almost standard procedure, if you think about it. Surely your doctor and oncologist have said the same before starting every treatment."

"What are the odds like, for failure, at each point?" asked Trey.

"Over the years, ABJ has lost just a handful of people during the conversion. But it's not easy to quantify, given that each case is different, and those numbers can be misleading. Someone in robust health, like you, will have a much higher rate of success. Why don't we focus on the number of BBs thriving for long periods of time?"

At this point, Arianne jumped in with more questions. "Where does a BB get its energy from? Could someone trace his whereabouts digitally? Why isn't ABJ more widely known and advertised?"

Finn walked into the room just then. "Good questions, Arianne," he said. "So how about we spend some time this Friday afternoon to go over all that. I'll invite my colleague. Look for an invite from me."

"That'd be helpful. Thanks," Arianne said.

Trey and his family thanked the team and left. Walking away from ABJ, the four of them were silent for a few blocks. Chase walked very close to his sister.

"What did you think about it, honey?" Val asked, her voice barely audible. She linked arms with Trey at their elbows and leaned toward him.

"I don't know," he replied quietly.

"I'm scared," Chase said to Arianne. She pulled him close.

"I know, but many people have done this already," she said. "It'd be like Dad was going on a trip, checking in on us, talking all the time. He'd definitely have more time to talk to you."

"But never really coming back?" Chase said.

"We wouldn't see him like this." As she uttered those words, she felt a lump in her throat.

"Like those people we see on the street sometimes, in orange jumpsuits? But Dad's brain will be at ABJ?"

"You mean the people in orange jumpsuits with VR goggles? They have done bad things. You know, people that commit crimes? So the prison punishes them by controlling where they can go and what they can see, through those goggles. They have very few places they're allowed into. They might be on the street here, but what they see is something totally different."

"Can they take their goggles off?" Chase said.

"No, that would send an alarm to the police immediately," Arianne said. She wondered about the parallels between the virtual worlds, one mandated by a prison and the other by cancer.

Even though he was staring down death, Trey continued to be apprehensive about the conversion for many days.

Late one night, Trey was tossing in bed, struggling to fall asleep. His scalp felt a little weird. Stumbling into the bathroom for a drink of water, he looked in the mirror. Many springs poked radially out of his scalp with a small electronic chip attached to the end. "Aaargh, aargh!" he screamed.

"Trey! Trey!" Val said as she reached over in bed, shaking his arm. "You okay? Did you have a nightmare?"

"Ha! Mmmphh. Strings. . . springs," he mumbled, stroking his hair. "Yeah."

He hugged her close.

"How could Fiona be interested?" he said to Val one day while shaving in the bathroom. "She's doing well. Ya know, she doesn't appear to have a reason?"

"Why don't you ask her?" replied Val, carrying some clean towels in.

Trey called Fiona later that day. She was at peace with her decision. But he was surprised when she turned the question back on him.

"Pardon me if I come out too blunt," she said. "As you say, your options are limited and time's running out. Are you leaning toward more treatment?"

"No, not really."

"I've seen neuralware implants work, and it's fantastic! We saw the awakening the other day. Didn't someone say some new technology is coming along to have a BB inhabit a whole bionic body? If that's what you're missing."

It was nothing Trey hadn't heard before, but strangely he felt hope, however slim. He felt a bit lighter.

Shortly after, one evening, as the Primeson family was busy running around getting ready to attend a cousin's wedding, Val went to Arianne for help with her own hair. Walking back to her room, she was lost thinking about how quickly her daughter had grown up into a beautiful, gorgeous woman.

Out of the blue, Trey said to her from across the room, his tone matter-of-fact and dispassionate, "Val! I believe I am ready."

She knew exactly what that meant. Trey Primeson had decided to go through with the conversion.

"We'll figure this out," she said, "together." She stood, stroking the bristles of her hairbrush, wishing time would stop so they could discuss it, dwell on the decision, give it the gravity it deserved.

Trey raised his hand. "For now, no more about it. We're going to enjoy this wedding, dance, and squabble with family like normal people."

"Sure. Sure," Val said. She wasn't exactly sure.

"If we are to survive this ordeal, let's practice by putting it off our minds this evening," he said.

"Well then," she said, smiling, "I recommend you behold the beauty in the room down the hallway before the squabbles begin." They both walked over and stood by Arianne's door.

"What?" Arianne said. "Why do you both have that look?"

"She's been painting her face all evening!" Chase said as he ran into Arianne's room.

"You little . . . ," Arianne said as she got up and chased after her brother.

"Oh my, we're late!" Val said. They all hurried out to the pod that had been summoned.

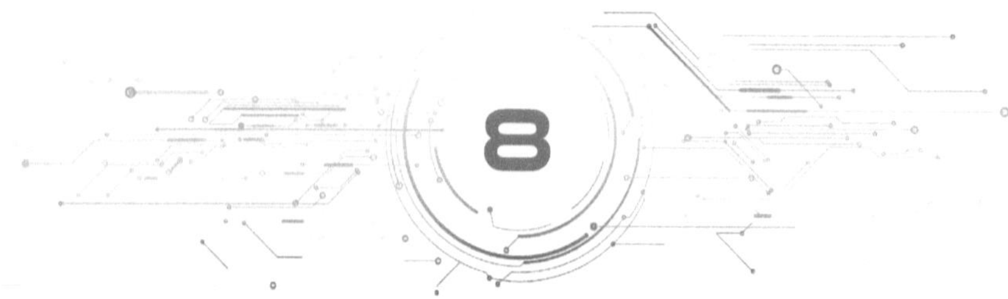

Finn took Trey into the BB room for his first visit. A few steps into the room, Trey was overcome by an uneasy feeling and a barely audible hum that got louder as he approached the tower of BBs. Having made *the* decision already, he fought his first instinct to flee. Fear gave in to exhaustion, more from the cancer consuming him from the inside.

"Would you like to sit?" Finn said. "Here." He pulled one of the chairs closer. Trey grabbed the chair and plopped into it.

"Quiet. Can you hear them think?" said a sign right next to the BBs. Finn sat in a chair and rolled the familiar test portal close to Trey.

BBs were housed in a large circular enclosure in the middle of the ABJ facility. Each BB, including their housing and connections, occupied about two cubic feet of space. Somewhere between eighty and a hundred BBs were arranged in circular, floor-to-ceiling tiers, each larger than the one below. A thick white conduit connected each BB straight up to a glass ceiling. The floor above looked like a chemistry lab. On the floor in the BB room were a couple of robotic assistants and several movable display monitors with attached hardware. A door led to the fabrication room for neuralware, which was situated toward the back of the building.

"You might remember some of this from the other day," Finn said, pointing to the test portal, which was just like the one used with BBGlen during the awakening Trey had witnessed. "Your family will have a portal just like this. Once a BB answers the call from the portal, you have a dedicated communication line. The BB feels as if they're physically here with us. They can receive sensory input: they can see, touch, hear. You are a techie, you'll like this." Trey sat up. "The BB is essentially connected, on demand, to the freeNet with the ability to communicate with any other devices on the freeNet. All communication to and from the BB is digital. In the digital realm, a BB is no different from a human connected through an electronic device. It can interact with and participate in the world just like a regular person would, accessing content from any website, making audio calls, sending and receiving messages using any social media platform. Digital input including audio and video is fed directly to the brain for processing. All output from the BB is directed to the intended electronic port, specifically chosen by the BB," Finn said.

Finn continued to explain that once surgery for the conversion was performed successfully and the neuralware had had time to establish connections with the brain, the BB was pretty much self-sustaining. Neuralware made the critical connection between the brain and the electronic ports that were used for digital input and output. Core software that a BB needed to function was self-correcting and self-evolving.

Downloads of new software, communication ports, and connections with other devices were initiated and approved by the BB as needed.

Trey just listened. He had forgotten the many questions that he had been mulling over the past couple of days.

Trey made regular visits to ABJ. There was so much to obsess about. Every small detail and bit of data coming out of every system was reviewed by at least three team members. He was intimately involved at every step. The psychologist suggested that it would play a critical role in how well-adjusted his BB was going to be after the conversion. He said it would be most beneficial for Trey to spend time in the room full of BBs to come to terms with what he would soon become. He was encouraged to talk to BBs using the test portal.

Weeks went by, and Trey's entire world seemed to shrink and shrink, until it was confined within the walls of ABJ. When he wasn't at home, he was at ABJ, talking to the other BBs.

"You haven't eaten anything," Val said one morning as Trey was getting ready to leave.

"Not hungry, I'll be back soon," Trey said.

"You say that, but you didn't come home until dinner yesterday," Val said. Trey just mumbled something and left.

Chase was helping around the house more, especially with the greenhouse. He had stopped horsing around and was instead keeping to himself and even brooding sometimes. Arianne decided to work from the family's home more often.

She moved many of her things back from her apartment. Early one morning, she found Val standing in the kitchen, mug in hand, staring out the window.

"Where's Dad?" Arianne said.

"He didn't come home last night," Val said, worried. "I just messaged Maya."

"Chase?" Arianne called out.

"He's in his room, working on a project," Val said, still standing in front of the window.

A few moments later, the phone rang, and Val answered. "Hello?"

"Val? This is Maya. I have Dr. Sagan here, one of the psychologists."

"Doctor, he didn't come home last night. Is Trey losing his grip on reality? He seems to be detaching himself from the family."

"But that's precisely what we want," Dr. Sagan said. "Opening up his world after the conversion would be easier than confining it. You'll all pick up your relationships where you left off and rebuild connections after."

Val nodded as Dr. Sagan assured her that the team was keeping a close watch on Trey and that he was making good progress. Maya explained to her that some of Trey's own stem cells had been extracted earlier and were being used to grow neurons, which would then be fused with organic electronic components to build neuralware.

"After receiving the final approval from the testing team, we'll call the development of neuralware complete and hand everything over to the surgeons. That should happen soon," Dr. Sagan said.

As the big day drew close, it became clear that Trey wanted to avoid drama. Whenever Val remarked about something happening for the last time, he brushed it aside. He didn't want a fuss and a send-off on the big day.

"This isn't a trip to the dentist," Val said. "At a minimum, your mom is joining us."

And just like that, the day had come. Trey had a spring in his step as he woke up, went around petting Misha, checking in on the greenhouse, and getting some coffee. It was time for Trey to say goodbye to his reflection in the mirror. He had already sent all the hardware he had used for work back to his company, and the desk looked empty and clean as never before.

At every turn, Val couldn't help thinking, *That's the last time he's going to do that.*

He went into the bathroom and started shaving.

"How're you feeling?" Val said.

"I'm fine," Trey said.

"Great. You look great," Val said. She ran out of the bathroom in tears to bury her face in a pillow.

"Val! I thought you were . . . ," Trey said as he rushed to her. They hugged for a while until Trey felt too weak to stand. They sat down on the bed. Val saw the energy drain from his face. She got up quickly.

"No," she said. "We're going to make this work. We'll all be fine. Most importantly, you won't be in pain anymore." Trey nodded. "Arianne's been making something special for us this morning."

Trey put on a bright summer shirt. He and Val went down for breakfast. Chase was laying the table. Arianne brought a pie out of the oven. Chase looked around and left the room. He came back in after a moment, carrying Misha. They all sat around the table.

"All my favorites," Trey said. "Is Mom coming there directly?"

"She's coming there with my parents," Val said. "Apparently you told her not to make a big deal out of this."

"It isn't a big deal," Trey said. "Pass me the water, Chase." He tried to get Misha into a conversation. The cat jumped up on the windowsill. Several minutes of silence followed as Arianne watched Val just cut up a muffin into pieces and push them around with her fork. Chase ate like he was following instructions.

"You're going to be up in three months?" Chase asked, not looking at anybody in particular.

"I'll come under that. I'm strong, buddy," Trey said, trying to jab Chase's arm.

"So Maya asked us to come a little early if we could," Val said.

"Let me get all this put away," Arianne said, getting up.

"Don't worry about it. Just cover the pie," Val said.

They were all ready to leave.

"I'll be back," Trey said, almost to himself.

"I think the pod is here," Val said, avoiding eye contact. Trey walked out the door with the rest of the family close behind.

Out on the street, Arianne wondered, *How many such wonderfully normal days did I miss noticing?*

The last time we all, my family, will be together, physically, Val thought.

Val got a message on her phone from the pod. Soon, they got on. Trey and Val sat on the front seat. He reached over and held her hand. Behind them, Chase sat next to his sister. Seeing his lower lip quiver, she slid closer to him and put her arm around his shoulders.

"It's going to be okay," she mouthed.

Trey opened his mouth to say something to Val but changed his mind. They all mostly looked out of the window during the entire ride to ABJ. After getting off the pod, Trey walked slowly, savoring each step, looking around. Val looked back to see where he was. Trey was standing beside Chase, smiling at him. But the little boy barely came up to Trey's hips. Overcome by confusion, Val stood motionless. She quickly realized she had a surreal moment when she saw Chase standing, almost as tall as herself, to her right. The little boy, who walked away holding his mom's hand, looked so much like Chase when he was two! Trey caught up with the rest of the family, his breathing becoming more labored.

They all stepped inside ABJ. Maya, Finn, and Dr. Sagan were in the lobby.

"He'll be right back with you," Maya said to them as she and Dr. Sagan whisked Trey away. The color drained from Val's face. She didn't expect for Trey to be rushed into this, not leaving time to say goodbye.

"You'll see him before he goes in," Finn said. "We're headed this way." He led Val, Arianne, and Chase into the surgery prep room where Trey's mom and Val's parents were already waiting. They all hugged each other.

"Trey's on a quick tour of the BB room," Finn said. "He knows a few people in there, so just chatting a little bit." He put his hands in his pockets and looked at the entrance. "Do you all have any questions?"

Arianne looked around. Chase stood right next to her. The grandparents mostly looked down. Her mom had a blank stare. Soon they heard voices. Wheeled in on an adjustable bed, Trey looked relaxed. The entire family gathered around him. Arianne thought her dad looked a little too happy, drugged.

"Val! Guys! C'mon. Everything will be fine," Trey said. "I could attend my own funeral whenever you're having it," he chirped.

"Not quite," corrected an ABJ team member. "It takes more than a few weeks for you to be up and running after the brain is surgically detached."

Val broke down, then walked away and sat on a chair. Her mom followed her to console and comfort. "I can't imagine, honey, but let's hope for the best," she said.

Arianne stood, hugging Trey's mom and Chase. Val's dad leaned over by Trey's bed.

"Young man," he said to Trey, "I know you got this."

"Thanks," Trey said.

Arianne's face looked ready to explode when Dr. Sagan, the psychologist, took her aside and looked firmly into her eyes.

"You've always been strong," he said. "Your mom needs you now more than ever. We knew you'd be the one to pull everybody through."

Arianne nodded, biting her lip. She saw her dad looking over the back of the chair at her mom. She walked closer to him.

"Dad," Arianne said. "She'll be fine. We'll be fine. We can't wait to talk to you soon."

Members of the ABJ team had been in and out of the room, taking notice of Trey's vitals on the display monitor, adjusting the levers on his bed so he lay flat, and making sure he was comfortable.

Val composed herself and walked over to give her husband a final hug. He kissed her on the cheek. The rest of the family followed, hugging and reassuring Trey. Arianne looked around for Maya or Finn. Neither of them came back into the room.

"Um . . . can I talk to Maya?" Arianne asked Dr. Sagan.

"Not sure where she is," Dr. Sagan said. "I'll let her know. We have another team that will work with you from here on. They'll be in touch. You all should receive regular updates."

A part of Arianne wanted to scream foul play and stop the conversion right there while there was still time. But she suppressed her paranoia.

"Until we meet again," Trey said. Those were his last words to his family as they were all led outside the room.

Arianne called for a pod through her phone. A pod large enough for the extended family. On the ride home, the grandparents remarked for a little while about everyday things: how the city had so many trees now, some large enough for birds' nests; how so many more people rode the moving walkways instead of pods; how they had seen the city transform from being polluted and crowded by vehicles. Then everybody fell silent. Once home, they sat in the living room. Several moments of tense silence passed.

"Now how long did they say the first phase would take?" Val's dad said.

"You mean until the . . . separation?" Val's mom said.

"Several weeks," Arianne said. "They start on the brain implants right away, but the body is intact to help stabilize the neuralware." They all sat in silence.

Arianne thought about what they were told at ABJ. "During this initial period, it is quite unnecessary to duplicate what the body does best naturally—fuse, connect, and heal," they were told. "Another way to think about this is like a premature baby developing under medical attention at a hospital." Dr. Sagan also advised them not to rush into funeral arrangements considering it was hard to predict exactly when the brain would be detached from the rest of the body.

As advised by ABJ, during the following weeks, Arianne, Val, and Chase stayed as busy as possible in their own lives. Val woke up frequently at night with bizarre dreams. She couldn't go back to sleep thinking about all the what-ifs from the failure scenarios Maya and Finn had gone through. One time she had a nightmare similar to Trey's fears about being trapped in a video game.

Meanwhile, regular updates from ABJ continued:

Neural implantation complete. Vitals stable.

Neural functions back to normal.

Testing reception of sensory input and output.

Reception of sensory input and output successful.

Rerouting carrier fluid from external source. When Arianne saw this one, she ran to her mom.

"Mom, did you see the latest message?"

"What's carrier fluid?" Val said, looking over the display from her computer on the breakfast table. "Some of their messages are hard to understand." She took another sip from her coffee mug as her eyes went back to the display.

"So it carries oxygen, glucose, minerals, hormones—everything," Arianne said. She stood with a blank expression. Suddenly Val looked up. The mug almost slipped from her hands.

"Does this mean," Val said, "it's all done?"

"No," Arianne said. "It's just starting. Let me message Maya." After a moment she got an answer back. "Maya says things are looking good, but we'll get notified when the rerouting is successful."

Several hours later, they received another message that the cut over was successful.

A little while later, Val was in her bedroom on the phone. "Mom?"

"Val! What's going on?" Val's mom said. "Your father and I were about to call you."

"We um . . . need to arrange for . . . ," Val said.

"Is everything okay? Is Arianne with you?" Val's mom said. She messaged Arianne separately.

"The cut over was a success," Val said. "His brain doesn't need his body anymore."

"Don't worry about the funeral arrangements," Val's dad said. "Leave all that to us."

"I don't know how I'm going to . . . ," Val said, her voice fading. She sat on the bed. Arianne came into the room and sat beside her.

"Grandma? Grandpa?" Arianne said. "I'm here."

"Arianne, take care of Mommy," Val's mom said.

Later, Arianne spoke to her grandparents about how Trey's body and face would be put back together after the surgery. "You won't be able to tell," Maya had said.

Announcements were made of Trey's death due to cancer and of the funeral. Val sat by herself the night before the funeral, reading messages from extended family, friends, and people that had worked with Trey. Everybody expressed shock, sadness, and support for the family. Colleagues had written about how accomplished Trey was as a hardware engineer and how his work would help further satellite technology and also the automation of indoor agriculture. *I can't wait for him to see all these*, thought Val, looking at the largely empty bed. She wondered if Trey was conscious at that moment. Soon, the sun shone through the window. Val darkened the window tint from the controls by her bed.

"Mom, are you up?" Chase knocked on her door.

"Come on in, Chase," Val said. Chase sat on the bed. Val put her arm around him. They sat in silence for a little bit.

"Is Dad . . .going to be there?"

"Yes," Val said. "He'll look the same." Arianne heard them talking and went in and sat at the foot of her mom's bed.

"Chase," Arianne said, "we're not supposed to say anything to anybody about BBs."

"I know," Chase said. "Is it okay if I don't want to see him?"

"See whom?" Arianne said.

"He means Dad," Val said calmly.

"You mean Dad's body?" Arianne said.

"Is it, Mom?" Chase said.

"If that's what you want," Val said.

"Can I wear a yellow shirt, Dad's favorite color?" Chase said.

"Sure, whatever you want," Val said. She got off the bed. "I think we should get going."

Arianne went up to the windows and adjusted the tint back to let in the bright sunshine.

⁂

At the funeral hall, Val felt sick to her stomach as she approached Trey's body. She gripped Arianne's arm tightly. Feeling suddenly drained of energy, Trey's mom had to be helped to a chair.

"You know he's at ABJ," Arianne whispered, expressionless.

"How could it be? All of him is right there," Trey's mom said.

Chase sat next to Trey's mom, his nose red, his eyes looking down.

Visitors began pouring in. Arianne and Val stood in front of Trey's body, talking to them.

"If there's anything we can do," said one.

"So sorry for your loss," said another.

One after the other, the visitors viewed Trey's body, offered help, and wished Val and Arianne courage.

Back at home that night, Val stepped into her bedroom. *What if this is really it?* she thought. She imagined Trey's brain in a bubble. *What if he can't be woken up? Or worse yet, the communication systems fail?* Not able to think of anything positive, she went into the hallway to see if Arianne was awake. The entire house was dark and very quiet. She went back to bed and lay there waiting for sleep.

Then, just like that, a few weeks later, a message from ABJ arrived: **Congratulations. Trey will be up on the 3D portal at ABJ.**

ABJ had performed exhaustive testing, and Trey was ready to meet his family for the first time on the 3D portal.

The family gathered in ABJ's lobby. Chase and Arianne ran up to Trey's mom. Val hugged her.

"You look really tired, dear, have you not been sleeping well?" Trey's mom said.

Val smiled weakly.

"Let me find Finn or Maya," Arianne said, looking around. She messaged them.

"Everything will go fine," Trey's mom said. "Feels like the day baby Trey was born."

"Baby Trey or BBTrey?" Chase said.

"Yes!" She nodded and smiled at Chase.

Soon they were led into the same room where they had witnessed BBGlen awake. Maya was there.

"The hard part's over, isn't it?" Arianne said.

"Let's hope so," Maya said. "And I'm sorry I've not been too responsive. Been crazy busy here."

Finn and a couple of his colleagues were preparing the stage up front. Arianne went closer to the stage.

"Hi, Arianne. How're you all doing?" Finn said.

"Fine, I guess," Arianne said. "Just anxious."

"I can imagine," Finn said. "Even for us, every time we awaken a BB, it feels like the first time. From here, we see all of you, all the emotions you feel."

Arianne heard someone calling for Finn's attention.

"I guess I'll let you go," she said.

Arianne joined Val, Chase, and Trey's mom, who were seated in the front two rows. Val was reminded of the time she sat waiting for BBGlen to wake up. When it ended abruptly in failure. When she and Trey thought they were never going through with the conversion. Now she found herself literally holding her breath. The portal was fired up. The four of them leaned forward. Trey's 3D hologram appeared, but it seemed static.

"Trey?" Finn called. Everybody waited, motionless.

"Yeah?" the voice from the portal said. Almost in a whisper. There was a slight movement in the lips.

"Can you hear us fine?" Finn said.

"Yes, I can," said the voice again. More audible this time. More like Trey. The head and face of the 3D hologram moved as he spoke. The four of them leaped forward as close to the stage as possible.

"Dad!"

"Trey!"

"Honey!"

There were no strangers watching in the room, and they felt comfortable being themselves.

"Dad! Dad!" Chase said, holding up a screen with a video clip from his baseball game from the week before. "Wink if you can see it?"

BBTrey smiled.

"Are you tired?" Trey's mom and Val asked at the same time.

"More disoriented than tired," BBTrey said.

"Can you see all of us?" Arianne said.

"Yes," BBTrey said. The hologram turned, and his eyes tracked the people around him.

"He needs time to practice using all the different ports for sensory input and software uploads," Maya said.

"Takes me a bit of concentration and conscious effort to switch between the real world and VZones," BBTrey said.

After testing the 3D portal and messaging and calling him directly, the family returned home. A couple of engineers from the ABJ team went with them to install a 3D portal at home.

Over the next few weeks, Trey struggled to adapt. Communicating was like learning a new language all over again. Before the conversion, he'd scoffed at the thought of reaching out to a shrink, but now he depended on Dr. Sagan to help him cope with his new form. The psychologist was coaching him on methods of visualization and a specialized form of meditation. Like traditional meditation, a BB had to train to achieve focus and inner balance. Each task took a lot of effort.

"Think of how a baby learns to talk," Dr. Sagan said.

"I'm trying," BBTrey said. "But it's different as an adult; I feel exhausted all the time."

"That's normal," Dr. Sagan said. "You've been awake for less than a week. Be sure to use the sleep cycle to rest up."

"That's how I've made it this far," BBTrey said.

"Don't use it as a crutch, though," Dr. Sagan said. "If you give up on communicating with the world and participating in VZones, you'll end up an isolated ball of neurons. Sleep only when you're prompted by the system messages."

Val turned on the 3D portal at home. BBTrey's hologram was static. "Trey?"

"Mmmmphpph," BBTrey said. "Wasn't there another cancer treatment I hadn't tried?"

"Treatment?" Val said.

"It's impossible. Had I known, I wouldn't have done this."

"Don't, Trey! Give it some time."

"Easy for you to say."

"Arianne wanted to talk to you. She'll be here later."

"I need to turn on the sleep cycle now." BBTrey wanted to avoid another exhausting conversation that resulted in mental fog and frustration. "Try me after an hour and a half."

BBTrey didn't turn on the sleep cycle. Instead, he decided to search the freeNet for the latest treatments for his cancer, just to make sure he didn't miss a promising cure. With great difficulty, he figured out how to invoke the sensor to send digital output, and he sent a few medical terms he remembered from his days of treatment. Lo and behold, search results popped up. To his surprise he could read every web page almost instantly. Just like seeing and hearing, he could make sense of the digital input directly. It was like feeding data to a computer program. Before long, BBTrey had taught himself the basics of communicating over the freeNet.

"Really? You mean you can read the news, see the pictures, and make sense of it all?" Val asked over the 3D portal.

BBTrey went on to explain how he could access any website and get a digital feed of the content uploaded to his BB.

"Almost instantly," he said with a big smile.

Val let out a big sigh of relief.

"I'm so sorry," BBTrey said. "I can't believe I was so caught up about why I went through the conversion at all. I guess I've been fighting this."

"Are you kidding? The psychologist was amazed at how quickly you're adjusting to the transformation."

"Really? But we saw BBGlen up and running immediately."

"Well, didn't he have a big hiccup when they tried the first time?" Val said. "Took him weeks!"

She went on to update him about all that was happening at home: how Arianne decided to move back into town, which was immensely helpful, and about how Chase loved horsing around with his sister and was happy to have her around.

"I'm worried about Arianne," Val said. "She's so capable. I really thought projects would start pouring in after that award."

"The first big project is going to be key," BBTrey said. "Didn't she make connections at the award ceremony?"

"She did," Val said. "Nothing panned out."

"She's young," BBTrey said. "Give it some time."

BBTrey discovered that the freeNet searches he had done were merely scratching the surface. Any broadcasted or telecasted content on the freeNet was accessible to him. He was connected to the world and all the electronic devices at the family's home. While it was wildly entertaining to turn the hose on Chase and spook the family pets with beastly roars, he had to be careful when and where he played his pranks if he didn't want to risk being discovered.

Chase was especially excited about putting Dad's new "superpowers" to good use as Arianne had a friend coming over for the weekend. "Dad, can you listen in on the home speaker system?" he pleaded. "After they go upstairs, they won't know. Just think of all the stuff I'd find out. I could sell tickets to my friends!"

"No, don't torture your sister." BBTrey smiled.

"How about making hissing and squeaking noises in the middle of the night?" Chase said.

Though Chase didn't get his wish there, BBTrey did turn the electronically controlled sprinklers on when Arianne and her friend were in the greenhouse as Chase watched. BBTrey became increasingly comfortable interfacing with various devices. The following week, he got to watch Chase's soccer match as if he was right there on the bleachers. Late one night, he detected an attempted cyberburglary on the home network, then thwarted the attempt and alerted the family. Arianne raised their cybershield and reported it to the authorities. *Perhaps I can even find purpose being a BB*, he thought.

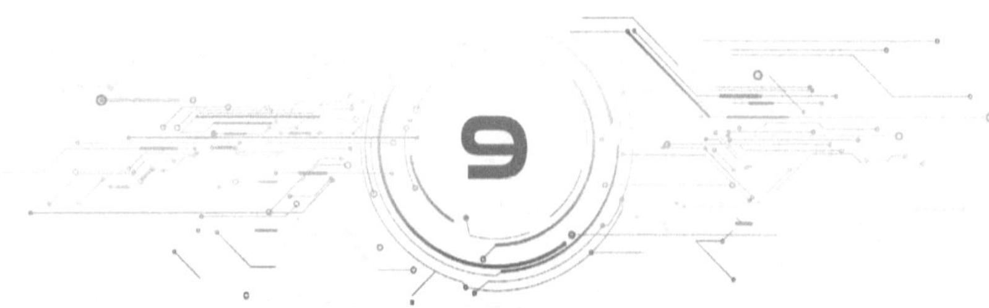

Not too long after watching BBGlen's awakening, Fiona made her decision. She found the adventure and the lure of "forever" hard to resist. She remembered how it felt to have been passed over for the project on the far side of the moon a few years earlier. To her, ABJ was offering the otherworldly vacation she'd always dreamed of. "How soon were you thinking?" Simona asked as they sat in Fiona's living room.

"I'm getting offers for the gallery," Fiona said.

"Wow, that soon, huh?" Simona said. "What about Jeeves?"

"Thoughts on being a hand-me-down, Jeeves?" Fiona jokingly said to her butler bot.

"If you're referring to transferring ownership . . ." The bot went on with instructions on how one might accomplish that, including contacting AmieBots for recycling and repurposing.

"I hope you understand why I'm doing this," Fiona said.

Simona nodded. "I can't imagine not having you."

"Don't you see? That's why I'm doing this," Fiona said. "Join me after a few years. Forever."

So it was settled. Fiona was ready for the next phase of her life. Her close family would know about her conversion and the physical whereabouts of her BB, but for everyone else, her digital persona and interaction would have to suffice.

"What should we say to people who insist on a personal meeting?"

"Just say, 'She's really not open to visitors these days. Become kind of reclusive. You know how that goes.'"

"Can we trust ABJ?" Simona said.

"I haven't found a reason not to," Fiona said.

"Absence of evidence," Simona said, "doesn't mean evidence of absence."

"I understand," Fiona said, "but Jeeves and I have done extensive searching. We're fine. They are not into anything secretive."

"I sure hope so," Simona said.

Fiona announced that she was selling the gallery to retire to an island in the Antarctic. Nobody was surprised about her destination. The news just magnified the intrigue surrounding her.

Scores of friends, fans, and colleagues came to the farewell event at the gallery. She was inundated with questions:

"My dear, you're leaving a big void in our world. Whatever are we going to do?"

"What's your next project? Is there any way we can get news on your activities?"

"Are you moving to Mars?" said one little girl as her mom tried politely to shush her. "My mom says you belong on Mars."

In her short farewell speech, Fiona promised everybody she'd keep in touch and send glimpses of her exciting new life.

Fiona had many weeks to prepare herself mentally for a virtual future. Talking with BBs through the 3D portal at ABJ revealed a lot of exciting opportunities for her, both in the virtual realm and the real world. ABJ arranged for her to participate in one of the BBZones, a virtual group for BBs so she could talk to whichever BB had time and was willing. BBGlen was among the first BBs she wanted to check on. All seemed well with him, which gave Fiona some comfort. Her third time in the BB room at ABJ, she initiated the connection and Trey's hologram came up on the portal.

"Hi, Trey. It's been a while."

"Wait, Fiona?" BBTrey said. "What brings you here? You thinking of doing the conversion?"

"I am. How've you been? How did it go?"

"The conversion itself was a success, I guess. Here I am," BBTrey said. "The couple of weeks after I woke up were tough. But now I can't imagine any other way. It's so much fun; I hardly have time to sleep."

"That's great!" Fiona said. "What are you into? What's your day like?"

"There's no typical day, as such. I'm in several VZones. You know about the ones for our families. I hate to admit it, but it's more fun in the BBZones. Each one has a different theme. It's nice to meet the same people and have discussions. They're like old friends now. We have a lot of physical activities, too. So, yeah, these last couple of days, I went skiing and saw the aurora—the actual live feed from a camera, not the VR version."

"Could you tell the difference?" Fiona asked.

"I'd like to think so. Besides, why develop VR for what's available as a live feed?"

"Makes sense," Fiona said. "But when you go skiing, is it just visual?"

"Oh no," BBTrey said. "I actually feel like they're my legs, I feel the bump when I go over something."

"So it's not like a video game," Fiona said.

"Funny you should say that," BBTrey said. "That was my fear, too. No, it's not like that. Feels like . . . real life."

Fiona sat nodding and listening to BBTrey.

"Now I'm trying to get into research," BBTrey said. "On neuralware. I have a few new applications in mind. I attend discussions to shape policy for sentencing criminals. As BBs, I think we have a unique perspective."

"I had no idea," Fiona said, "you could keep yourself so busy."

"Absolutely," BBTrey said. "There's so much we can do. Although, to be honest, in the beginning, all I did was enjoy the freedom. I literally had nobody and nothing standing in my way. I never felt so . . . unrestrained."

Fiona raised her brows. "Unrestrained?"

"I'm aware of the irony," BBTrey said. "Think zero answerability, zero responsibility." His hologram smiled. "Did I convince you yet?"

"Oh, I *am* doing this. In the next couple of weeks here."

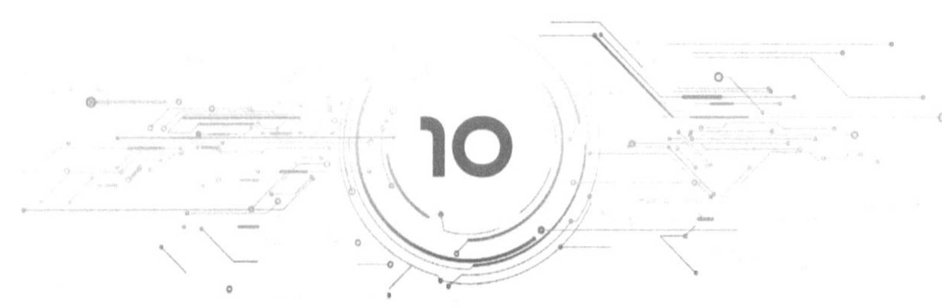

10

The Primesons were getting adjusted to Trey as a BB. Between school and sports, whenever Chase found time, he spent more time in the greenhouse. Trey taught him how to operate the controls and recognize emergencies. Val was working on a new project. Her team was developing a synthetic liver that was capable of filtering nanoscale and microscale plastics. She wondered if it could've cured or prevented Trey's cancer. As a freelance software engineer, Arianne was still struggling to land projects in her area of interest—artificial intelligence. Although she did most of her work remotely, she had some occasional travel. Trey could've been on a long trip out of town—leaving everything around the house otherwise unchanged. A trip with no return date.

Trey kept himself occupied. Some days were just for his own entertainment and enrichment, but he did enjoy volunteering in the freeNet community. He signed up to help as long as he didn't have to reveal his identity. As did several of his fellow BBs.

Late one afternoon, Trey came out of a sleep cycle to a message in the BB Zone: **We deeply regret to inform you that** one of your community is no more. We've lost BBLaurie. All processing in her bubble stopped as of two this morning. None of her input sensors picked up any signals. All vitals routinely monitored from the bubble seemed within normal range. Our engineers spent hours investigating, tracing communications in and out. The team that was studying the neurochemistry within the bubble noticed evidence of amyloid plaques, similar to those found in the brains of people with dementia. There hasn't been enough published research on how amyloid proteins affect neuralware. We choose healthy individuals for conversion to BBs—no one who has ever had any neurodegeneration. After converting to a BB, normal aging of the brain ceases, so there's no scope for developing plaques. Please be assured that our engineers have identified the biomarker involved and added it to the list of monitored parameters. We have also uploaded the necessary software to all the BBs. We want to assure you that there is no cause for concern for the rest of you.

Trey called on the portal at the family's home. Nobody answered. He knew nobody would be home that early, but he tried anyway. Val saw the notification on her phone.

I should be home in an hour. Call you then? All fine? Val wrote back.

Val got home and called Trey through the 3D portal.

"Remember Laurie?" Trey asked. His facial expression on the portal and the tone of his voice gave Val a knot in her stomach.

"BBLaurie? The amateur astronomer? Trey, what happened?"

"She failed to respond late last night. Last time her family talked to her was two days ago, and everything seemed normal."

"Really?" Val said, her brows raised. BBTrey read out the message they received in the BBZone.

"There were no signs of distress in any of her messages. They've lost BBs during the conversion but not. . . BBLaurie had been healthy for many months. Do you think we were too hasty?" BBTrey said.

"Don't go there again," Val said. "This could be an anomaly, a one-off event. Let's not panic. Don't second-guess—you didn't have much time left with the cancer. Did ABJ say exactly how this happened?"

"Not more than the message we all received," Trey said.

"Have they lost anyone before?"

"That's the thing. None of us had ever heard of it happening before, but maybe ABJ just didn't tell us about these disasters. Could they be using us for testing?"

Val wished Arianne was around. "Testing? Do the other BBs think that, too?"

"Well, Fiona's quite shaken. The others have been here a lot longer. But the BBZone is on fire—there's nothing else we talked about all day."

"How's your volunteering going?"

"It's going well. I got Fiona to sign up, too. I can't explain it, Val," BBTrey said. "Laurie was quite normal when she communicated until the end. She was working on a massively distributed computing effort for deciphering radio signals from a faraway galaxy. That's not something you can do with a degenerating brain."

"Perhaps it's just a rare occurrence," Val said. "Oh, before I forget, Chase had a question about the nutrients in the greenhouse."

"Yeah," Trey said. "He has to maintain a steady pH. I showed him how. He'll get the hang of it. Wish I could . . ." BBTrey paused.

"Wish you were here, too," she said. Then she gestured at the portal with her hands. "But imagine if we didn't have this."

"Yes," BBTrey said. "But this is exactly what I was trying to avoid—not being around like my dad."

"Don't beat yourself up," Val said and smiled. "One day, I'll be telling our grandchildren about where people go when they get old. No more questions about what happens when we die."

"I'll be right here," BBTrey said.

"Yes you will," Val said. "It'll be the new normal. Happily ever after starts after you become a BB."

BBTrey smiled.

"Connect me to the BBZone," he said.

"You're still with me, Trey," Val said.

"Ha, sorry," BBTrey said. "I thought I ended the session. They were talking in the BBZone about an event at a funeral home for Laurie."

"Funeral home?" Val said. "A real funeral. . . is her family doing this?"

"Oh no," BBTrey said. "This is in the virtual realm. Real for us, though."

"Of course, of course," Val said. "Go ahead then. Love you, honey." She commanded the portal to hang up.

"Love you, too," BBTrey said.

Then he connected to the BBZone. There was an "in-avatar" event created for BBLaurie. Several of the activities in VZones involved audio- or text-only participation, but this time, BBTrey selected the option to attend the event in his own avatar. He was a bit late joining the rest of the avatars at the funeral home. He looked around at all the avatars of BBs, some of whom he had only spoken to before. He spotted Fiona sitting in one of the rows in the back, went over, and sat beside her.

"Where have you been?" Fiona said.

"An ill-timed sleep cycle, I guess," Trey said. "This looks more real than, you know . . ."

"Than the real world?" Fiona said. "Isn't that why we're here?"

Up front at the podium, some of the avatars eulogized Laurie. Some others got philosophical.

"This is the largest family I've been part of," one of them said.

"Every single avatar is here," Fiona whispered to Trey.

"Didn't realize there were so many of us," Trey whispered back.

Laurie's breakdown brought the BB community a little closer. Following the big funeral event, there was more participation in the VZones. Their avatars met and discussed more often in the BBZone. Before, most of the BBs wanted communication and connection with the physical world and the people in it, but now BBs started more VZones. They started forming deeper connections. Fiona was quite popular, with her dry humor and adventurous spirit. Trey enjoyed reliving his childhood by playing pranks in the real and VR world.

Having met as real people before their conversion, Fiona and Trey shared a special bond. They interacted with each other in the BBZone a lot and were heading an effort to help BBs become more relevant and useful to people in the real world, to go beyond the selfishness of just living forever, to find new purpose. Since ABJ was still shrouded from the public in a bit of secrecy, they joked about how they'd do this "after ABJ comes out." Fiona and Trey imagined a future where they could openly participate in the real world. The possibilities seemed endless—space exploration, research, surveillance, parallel computing, even rent-a-brain activities, to name a few.

11

rianne set out to visit a potential client. Unlike the other companies she had dealt with before, this outfit was in a town west of Manhattan. She left early enough to avoid the crowds as the sun was rising. The aboveground, high-speed rail connecting towns went over reforested areas with animal and bird life. With minimal human contact and inter-ference, nature was flourishing. Especially during sunrise, the view of the forests was spectacular. She sat down, looking out the windows. Her gaze slowly drifted across the aisle. Luca! She recognized him from the programming class years ago, the cool guy who always had the best solution for every problem, at least in his own estimation. He excelled in math and phys-ics and was widely known as sharp witted, with a tough-guy attitude, albeit a bit mean spirited. She still remembered the prank she played on him back then like it was yesterday. One day in class, he was bragging to a bunch of students about his exploits and how he had cleaned out other kids' wins in an online game. As soon as he left the room, Arianne got to work. She cleaned out his wins, chopped off his network avatar's head just above his eyebrows, and changed the status to "Smart enough to give myself a lobotomy." By the time Luca got wind of it, the network was exploding with e-laughter.

The next day, Ms. Perl invited her to help Luca optimize a program. She was so sure it was a setup. *Surely Ms. Perl found out it was me*, she had thought. Her heart thumping, Arianne had looked over his shoulder and suggested that he change a certain construct in his program. He dismissed the suggestion and was quite reluctant to entertain any of Arianne's ideas. But Ms. Perl urged him to try. Luca obliged, changed the code per Arianne's recommendation, and found that the program ran much faster in identifying a pattern he was searching for. Arianne remembered every bit of the conversation.

"Oh, that's one way to do it," he said.

Ms. Perl beamed.

"That was an ingenious work-around," she said to Arianne. "I'd love to see you participate more; I bet you could help some of the other students, too. Don't be shy."

"How uh . . . ," Luca started but checked himself.

"Yeah," she said. "I saw that your loop didn't include—"

"Right. Right. Of course. I just missed the . . . Arianne, is it?"

"Yes," she said.

"I'm Luca," he said. "Thanks. I'm running late; see you around."

Luca excused himself and made a dash for the exit.

Arianne smiled to herself, wondering if Luca still remembered the incident. She also remembered Ms. Perl encouraging students at the lab to use any IoT devices at home to practice on.

"You have to create your own projects," she said. "Don't worry about breaking something. Tickle your security system. Go start an argument between your refrigerator and your dishwasher! No matter what your line of work is, whatever your area of interest in life, this is the default medium of interaction with every device you'll encounter—toilets through particle accelerators. It's a critical skill."

That programming class way back had turned out to be so useful. She loved how she could hack her way through her dad's BB, giving him more access to the outside world than ABJ's software allowed. She even broke into some of the VZones he was part of in order to add some features. In the process, she gained invaluable insight into ABJ's technology and the engineering that went into making her dad's BB.

Sitting on the rail, Arianne smiled to herself and glanced at Luca from the corner of her eye. She wasn't surprised that Luca didn't recognize her. She wasn't the dorky, awkward teenager anymore. He had changed, too, but she was very good with faces. She reminded herself again that she wasn't the shy, dorky teenager.

"Luca?" she called.

"Hi, uh . . . ," he said.

"Arianne," she said. "From Ms. Perl's class." She regretted bringing up Ms. Perl's name. But he seemed friendly.

"Yes!" he said. "How've you been?"

After some pleasantries, they quickly went into the usual "You remember Ryan?" type of questions when they exchanged news about common friends. It was soon time to get off the rail. They decided to keep in touch. Arianne was relieved that the conversation ended right there with Luca. Ever since her dad had become a BB, it took effort to steer small talk away from any references to him, to be on guard and measure her responses. ABJ had coached the family to reel out a rehearsed explanation to anyone outside the inner circle of family and friends: "It's just a VR personality simulator of my dad that the grief counselors set up for us. I tweak it for fun. And also, my little brother is quite young. He probably still believes that Dad's alive. Just helps us cope, you know."

Available to the general public as a subscription service, a VR personality emulator analyzed conversations and messages from all media platforms and networks that a person had ever sent to develop deep AI and algorithms to mimic their personality for all forms of digital communication. Initiating conversation, replying to messages, offering help and guidance were some of the tasks the AI performed. The emulator proved very effective, especially for younger children who had trouble with the loss of a family member or friend: "I want to tell Grandpa about it." For adults it was a good coping mechanism: "Wish Aaron was here. What would he have said?" Emulators were getting so good in mimicking a person that it was getting harder and harder to prove authenticity. Companies had long been using them for online customer-facing roles.

That evening, Arianne was talking to her dad over the 3D portal when Chase interrupted.

"Back by popular demand," he announced, trying to bother his sister. "A round of wet willies on me!" He was growing bigger, but she managed to put him in a headlock.

"*Das ass! Das ass!*" Chase said, repeating the bit of German he'd learned that day. Arianne tightened the headlock.

"Dad! Daaaaackkk!" Chase made fake gagging noises.

"Chase! Do you want to watch your sister and learn to program?" asked BBTrey.

"No! Das ass," he said and galloped away, but he changed his mind and came back. "What do I get?" he demanded.

"You know Ms. Perl was my best programming teacher?" Arianne said. "She used to joke about pitting the dishwasher against the refrigerator. Bet I can put in a bug. Hey! How about I get the refrigerator to say, 'Chase loves Tonya' when you open the door?" Arianne laughed.

Chase stuck his tongue out at his sister. "Tonya is ugly. You're ugly."

"Wait, Dad, why don't I bypass the input to your voice-out for reading out a canned message? Yeah, Chase, how would you like that?"

"Dad, can you say that I'm the best? Can you do that, Arianne?" Chase said.

"Fine," BBTrey said. "But please be extra careful. Arianne, don't let him distract you. Don't wanna jam anything up—ABJ support fellas are going to be annoyed. They've been getting a bit strict these days."

"We'll be fine," Arianne said and turned toward Chase. "Best at what, Chase?"

"Just the best . . . at everything! At hacking!" he replied, nodding smugly.

"All right!" BBTrey said. "But what's the trigger, though? Don't want to be randomly bumbling about Chase being a good hack."

"Das ass!" Arianne said. "That's the trigger! When someone says, 'das ass,' your voice-out will reply, "Chase, you're the best hack the world has ever known.'"

It took a while for Arianne to figure out the hardware and for her and BBTrey both to keep a safe distance from the neuralware. He approved the upload of the software into his BB. She surprised Chase with the prank later that night with BBTrey on the 3D portal.

"Chase! How about some German?" she asked him.

"Das ass!" he said, only too happy to say it.

"Chase, you're the best hack the world has ever known," BBTrey's voice-out promptly replied. Then Chase wouldn't stop, which meant BBTrey repeated the message over and over. No matter what activity BBTrey was engaged in, the voice output occurred in parallel.

"Looks like all the hard work is finally paying off," Val said when she heard it, with a wink.

"It's like old times, isn't it?" Arianne said.

BBTrey smiled.

"Yeah," Val said. "Except that this boy here is becoming a handful." She tousled Chase's hair.

12

ost afternoons while Arianne and Val were busy, Chase talked to his dad. Inconceivable as it seemed, Chase was actually happy for the quality time. And it also helped Chase avoid being home alone. Today they were talking about family vacations. Ever since Trey's conversion, he had been "joining" the other three through a sensory phone. For Trey, it was like he was right there with them, seeing all the sights they were seeing, sharing the whole experience together. They even joked about how Trey didn't need any tickets or food, he was practically vacationing for free. On their most recent trip, they had gone to a secluded island in the Pacific. Chase liked the augmented reality version of diving and snorkeling with goggles that superimposed images of marine life, now mostly extinct. Arianne took part only occasionally, and he was quite upset that he didn't get to spend much time with her.

"This time I wanna go someplace without a beach," he said. Trey understood that he didn't like losing his sister to more mature pursuits than sandcastles and marine-life scavenger hunts.

"Well, I'm sure there're more rainforests," BBTrey suggested. "How about one high up in the mountains? You loved birding last fall, didn't you?"

"Fall?"

"Yeah, sometime last October."

"What rainforest?" he asked, confused while petting and bothering Misha, who had sauntered into the room. "We didn't go anywhere. Arianne didn't wanna miss her dumb performance."

Father and son argued about their disparate memories of the most recent family vacation, and it was soon time for Chase to get on with his evening.

"See you later, Dad!"

BBTrey's conversation with Chase got him wondering. His son wasn't so young that he wouldn't remember where they went just months earlier. He started to worry and thought of BBLaurie's death. Amyloid plaques! He could almost feel the plaques choking him.

Trey alerted the ABJ support team promptly. Neurologists went through their testing and concluded that there was no indication of plaques.

"What about the big discrepancy between our memories?" he asked.

"Even 'normal' people forget things often," Dr. Velasquez said. "And complicating matters is the virtual life, or many lives, you're involved in. Don't dwell on it. The technical team is monitoring the biomarker responsible for tracking amyloid plaques."

Val brushed it aside, too. "Jeez, Trey, we all forget things," she said. "I was at home wondering why it was so quiet until I remembered that I was an hour late to pick Chase up from soccer."

"It's understandable when you're productive," BBTrey said.

"Now, don't start that again!" she said. "We made the best decision. We're all adjusting to the new situation. Arianne's running almost everything around here. Sometimes I wonder what I'd do without her. And well, Chase is Chase . . . although he's not tormenting his sister as much as before." She laughed. "I suspect she misses that."

"Yeah. I guess. I'm not complaining about the conversion. Just wish ABJ was more open about it, and I didn't have to hide."

"Arianne tells me that's going to change," Val said. "Maybe not this year or the next, but she said soon you'll be able to sign up for projects and even apply for a job."

"Well, I hope she's right."

"Bye, honey," Val said.

Getting back to the practical part of their lives, Val remembered that she and Chase were going to visit the Mansours, one of the neighbors. Their daughter, Amira, Chase's friend, was recovering from an accident.

Val found Chase mucking around in the greenhouse.

"Honey, please wash up. Let's go visit them!" Val said.

"C'mon," he said. "They won't mind. Been there many times, her mom's really nice."

"I have to take a business call soon," Val said.

"Coming," Chase said.

"You take your call, Mom, I'll go with him," Arianne said.

Arianne and Chase went over. Waiting to be recognized by the cameras on the neighbor's porch, Arianne noticed twigs sticking out of Chase's pockets and a bit of mud on his pants and around the back of his shoes.

The door opened and they were ushered into a grand room straight out of the Victorian era. Mrs. Mansour was impeccably dressed head-to-toe in black except for an elegant line of gold embroidery around the neck. She was ultrapolite and so soft spoken that Arianne had to lean forward and concentrate to hear her. Everything about the lady and the house screamed "formal." Arianne tried to discreetly glare at Chase for his muddy pants. He frowned at her and darted to find his friend.

Amira was in a room near the back of the house. Her left leg was in a cast and extended straight, and she was in a robotic chair that helped her get around. Arianne inquired about the accident, and Amira was excited to tell the story. Arianne expressed concern, and Chase thought the chair was cool and made plans with Amira to use it for all sorts of antics. Walking back to the grand room, Mrs. Mansour invited them to be seated and brought coffee from the kitchen in exquisite china on a beautiful tray.

"Uh . . . uh . . . I . . . we . . . don't drink coffee . . . ," Arianne started to blurt, but seeing the expression on the lady's face, she decided it'd be too impolite to refuse. She tried to take a sip and almost gagged. Mrs. Mansour talked about the accident like a news anchor on TV, only in almost a whisper. She was sure that the recovery was progressing well. After a few moments, she left the room and reappeared with another gorgeous tray of cups and saucers.

"Arianne, you must prefer tea," she said. "And, Chase, you'll love these; they just came in." She presented a tray of individually wrapped chocolate desserts and thrust several of them into Chase's hands.

Initially, Arianne was embarrassed and apologetic about Chase's muddy clothes, but at this point she started to find the whole thing amusing. It was as though they were in a historical movie. Just to be polite, she ate one of the chocolates. After some more conversation, Arianne and Chase wished Amira a speedy recovery and said their goodbyes. Stepping out of the house felt like a leap into the future.

"What a sweet lady," Arianne said. "The chocolate was good; a little too heavy, though."

"I don't know," Chase said.

"Can stain your clothes," Arianne said, looking at his pockets.

"Can it stain sofa cushions?" Chase said.

"No," Arianne said, "you didn't."

Chase nodded. "I found other chocolates under there."

Arianne burst out laughing.

"Not the first victims, are we?"

"A good time-travel experience, Mom!" Arianne said, back home, as Chase told Val all.

"It's all good," Chase said. "The chocolates were wrapped."

For the first time in a long time, Arianne saw her mom laugh.

One evening later that week, Arianne was getting some work done when her mom peeked into the room.

"Busy?"

Sensing that her mom had something on her mind, Arianne tapped on a chair by the window next to her desk.

"Just finishing up something so I don't have to wake up too early in the morning."

Val walked in and sat. "Beautiful night, isn't it?"

"Yeah. Hey, how was the hike? Was it far away? Did you have to get a ride there?"

"A couple of pod rides away, not far at all. Some do it for the exercise, but I like meeting the people. Haven't been in a while; just didn't have the time."

"Really! A lot of people? Is it crowded?"

"Hardly, it's about eight that show up regularly. It's nice to see them face-to-face, you know." Val stared out into the moonlight with her chin propped up on her hand, lost in thought.

"Mom, is everything okay?"

"Yeah, yeah, everything's fine," Val said. "Some of us found a trail we hadn't been on before. It was wooded and lush."

"You know what I meant. Are you okay?" Arianne swiveled her chair around to face Val. "I'm not a child. I know you miss Dad, but this isn't about him, is it?"

Val sighed and looked at Arianne. "I loved spending the couple of hours forgetting everything, forgetting who I was supposed to be. It just doesn't feel right."

Clearly it wasn't exactly about the hike or the trail.

"What doesn't feel right?" Arianne said.

"Some of the people are really nice," Val said. "You know, everybody's understanding of our ordeal. But there's this guy who's especially supportive. I don't know . . ."

Arianne quickly turned to her computer. "Let me finish this real quick," she said, moving her finger on the track pad.

Val looked out of the window briefly and got up. "Oh my. I think I forgot to put the sauces away from dinner," she said. She came back after a few minutes.

"You were saying?" Arianne said.

"Oh, nothing that can't wait," Val said. "It's getting late."

"Uh . . . I'll be up for a bit," Arianne said, turning toward Val.

"That's okay. I'm off to bed."

Arianne pushed her chair away from the computer, propped her head on her chin, and stared at the screen.

Lying in bed, Val looked at Trey's side of her bed and ran her hand on his pillow. She thought to herself, *Didn't I encourage him to lock himself up in a small bubble? But here I am, ready to move on and have a life.*

Then she replayed the conversation from the hike in her head. They had broken off from the trail and went up a narrow path. They were soon enveloped by lush green vegetation. She looked around in delight.

"Is this real? So close to the trail, and we never knew."

"Getting lost has its advantages," he had said.

"Should we tell the others? The group has been missing out on all this."

After more lighthearted conversation, he asked how she had been getting on since her husband's passing.

"It's as expected," she said. "We knew . . . it was going to be hard."

"Ya know," he said, looking into her eyes. "There are many resources out there to help families. Especially when you had to deal with terminal illness."

"Thank you," Val said. "We're already working with a program. We're definitely more accepting of reality now."

"Healing takes time," he said, touching her shoulder.

On an impulse, she said, "Indeed. If you're . . . um . . . should we continue down this trail?"

He stepped forward eagerly. "Absolutely!"

Eternal life, connection with your family, and a rich virtual experience was the whole premise behind the BB. The uncomfortable and heretofore ignored conversation was looming large. Could she move on in this physical world? Even find a romantic partner? With her husband's transformation to a BB, she felt guilty about entertaining that thought. Would she have the time to continue her relationship with BBTrey? Wouldn't it become a chore at that point? BBs were supposed to make connections in the virtual world in addition to the ties with people in the physical world. So in a way, BBs were "moving on" in establishing their "forever." Mostly, she worried about what the kids would think, especially Arianne.

13

Ozzie deliberated a long time. AmieBots was encouraging employees to volunteer in labs around town to mentor students, but he had been putting it off. Independently run electronics and programming labs for all ages were cropping up all over cities, subsidized through charities and endowments. Companies received tax credits and used the opportunity for direct marketing and live demonstrations of their latest gadgets, gizmos, and devices. What better way to publicize their products than to have their employees demonstrate them and talk to potential customers? Many of the students wanted to play with the bots more than anything. Companion bots and housekeeper bots were the most popular of all. Eventually, Ozzie put his name in.

"Ozzie! You finally signed up," said Tomo, one of the office administrators, as he walked down the hall. "Thank you. You can visit a few before deciding, and I can send you a list of the labs, areas of concentration, and companies that mentor there."

Jamie, Ozzie's colleague, overheard. "What? Are you actually volunteering?" she said, winking at Ozzie. "I thought you didn't like people. Or was it just women? Or children?"

"Yeah, it'll be good for him to get out there," Tomo said. "Maybe you can show him around next time you go."

"I'm going this afternoon to the one on Vagus Street," Jamie said, turning to Ozzie. "Just a pod ride away, if you want to come along."

"Yeah, that would be wonderful," Ozzie said. "Can't wait to be with children."

Later that day as he and Jamie walked into the lab together, Ozzie started to explain. "I have no patience for unruly, hyperactive brats," he said.

"Weren't you a kid once?" Jamie said, smiling.

"Didn't have that luxury," Ozzie said, looking at the floor. "Grew up at a few homes."

"Oh, I'm . . . ," Jamie said, "sorry."

"There should be a tax for badly behaved children. For the parent, know what I mean?"

"Wake up, Ozzie!" Jamie said. "Students doesn't mean just children. Sure, I see some teenagers. They know so much, they'll probably take you for a spin. Watch out for the group at the workstation in that corner. You could talk to the ones joining the session virtually, if you prefer."

They stood looking around for a couple of minutes. The lab was busy, and the students hardly noticed them.

"Go ahead," Jamie said, heading to a group nearby. "Introduce yourself."

"Maybe later," said Ozzie, observing from a distance. After a while, he spoke to a couple of other mentors.

"I learned programming a few years ago at a lab just like this," Ada said.

"Really?" Ozzie said. "These things actually work?"

"Of course!" Ada said. "There're lots of talented students here. We're contacted by companies looking for apprentices or freelancers."

Over the next several days, Ozzie visited more such labs and signed up to mentor at one across town from AmieBots. Nobody from AmieBots had volunteered there yet.

His boss, Alex, had reluctantly allowed him to start the "holy shit" idea he'd come up with recently, so Ozzie truly did not have much spare time. Using deep artificial intelligence, he was developing a new robot to have a personality like that of an actual human being. It meant insane hours and late nights, sometimes in the back of AmieBots' labs—an area not accessible to many. And it required complete confidentiality. Competition had gotten fierce in this field. But still, he made time to volunteer at the lab. Within the first few days, he helped a few kids build circuits and develop software interfaces. Among them was Rami, a scrappy thirteen-year-old boy with a detached expression.

"I need to leave to pop into work for an hour or more," Ozzie said to Rami one evening in his usual brusque manner.

The boy nodded.

"Hey, you can go home," Ozzie said, getting up. "We can continue Friday if you want."

"I have time," Rami said. "I only go there to sleep."

Ozzie looked at him.

"I live in a foster home," Rami said.

"How long . . . ," he said. "How long have you been there?"

"As long as I can remember."

Ozzie sat back down. "Uh . . . I can stay a while longer," he said. He didn't leave until Rami left. After that day, Ozzie spent most of his time at the lab mentoring Rami. A fellow mentor noticed.

"Nice kid, isn't he?" she said, her curly red hair dancing as she spoke.

"Yeah, could've been me years ago," Ozzie said.

When he found that she had skills that complemented his own, he tried to get friendly with her. To his surprise, she didn't shake him off. Soon he was sneaking her into AmieBots and working with her on his latest project. He went to great lengths to let nobody at AmieBots know that she was involved. He sometimes invited her to work at his house, a combination of a lab and a filthy bachelor pad that was littered with all sorts of equipment. Well-dressed and tidy, she didn't fit in there. The first few times she had come over, he tried to clean the place, but he soon gave up. One evening, he heard the doorbell announce her arrival.

"Come on in," he called out.

"I never know what to expect, Ozzie," she said, looking at him and smiling ironically. He realized that he had nothing on but a medieval-looking robe.

"Oh, sorry. I meant to throw some pants on."

"I've seen it all," she said. "But thanks for trying to make a trail through the room for me." They laughed as she joined him in front of a big mess of electronic components and equipment on a table.

At AmieBots, Alex let him keep the technical details of the new project to himself and promised him that he could lead the development and launch.

"How's it going?" Alex said late one afternoon as Ozzie was just coming in. "Are you getting everything you need?"

"Absolutely," Ozzie said. "I was talking to marketing and customer relations. We're going to release the product at an international expo."

"Soon? Are we talking weeks?"

"More like months," Ozzie said. "I'll let you know. Going full speed, though. I'll be here late tonight."

"I hardly see you during the day. Nothing illegal is going on, I hope," Alex said, winking.

"Ha ha. Too funny," Ozzie said.

"If it is, just don't tell me," Alex said, laughing.

14

BBTrey spent a good part of the hour talking to Val on the 3D portal, relating news and events from the BBZone. He realized he was talking about BBFiona a lot and felt a little awkward.

"Trey! You have nothing to feel weird about," Val said. "I'm so glad you like her. She seemed pretty cool."

"Really," BBTrey said. "Hmmm."

"I mean that," Val said. "I care about you, but you shouldn't feel tied to the relationships just here in the physical world."

"But," he said, "the whole purpose of this was for you and me to be together. Forever or at least longer than the time cancer gave me. And I thought you'd eventually join me."

"Of course," Val said. "What do I know? We're not a normal family now. But we all care about each other. Don't you need fulfilling connections in both places?"

"Yeah, I guess so," BBTrey said.

"Oh, here's Arianne," she said. "I'll talk to you later, honey. Love you!"

He could hear Arianne's footsteps.

"Dad!" Arianne said, coming into view. "I'm using deep AI for my latest project." Arianne went on to tell BBTrey more about the project.

"That's fantastic," BBTrey said. "I wish Chase would learn from you."

"You know that boy is getting unmanageable these days," she said. "He's getting into everybody's business."

"He does seem to know a lot about what's going on in the greenhouse," BBTrey said.

"Apparently the servicemen said you taught Chase well," she said. "Of course they think he's taking care of it all by himself."

"I've got to start training him on it more," BBTrey said.

"Well, don't tell him I suggested it," said Arianne.

"Don't worry, I'll tell him you were no good at it. That's enough to get him interested," BBTrey said.

A new year dawned with several new BBs joining the BBZone. BBTrey was standing atop a ski slope on a VR mountain. BBTrey's avatar had a face in his likeness, but at the prime of his youth. The avatar's body was also youthful, dressed for surfing in swim shorts and a T-shirt. BBFiona appeared out of thin air, right next to him.

"Must be high up on everybody's New Year's resolutions," BBTrey said to BBFiona. "Did you hear about the number of incoming BBs?"

"Doubling, they said," BBFiona said. "Love your avatar, by the way." Her avatar was the image of her in her prime skiing days, in her youth, with cold-weather gear fit for the slopes. "I didn't think about losing the stuffy pants and jacket." She laughed. They both talked as they skied down.

"Do the engineers have the bandwidth to handle so many of us?" BBTrey said. A gentle breeze brought the smell of fir trees. A few flocks of geese flew high above their heads.

"I talked to Maya the other day," she said. "They're swamped trying to expand. Their staff has doubled since we converted, and they're still struggling to keep up with the work."

"I'm not surprised," he said. "Did she say anything about security?"

"Your attire says 'invincible,' but I'll ask anyway," BBFiona said with a laugh. They stopped at the bottom of the slope. "Should we be worried about security?" she said, looking at BBTrey.

"That's my biggest concern," he said. "I didn't mean to worry you, though."

"We just have to be on alert, I guess. You remember they started monitoring for another biomarker after losing BBLaurie. They need to be more proactive."

"They need to up the surveillance."

"I trust them," BBFiona said. "Everybody at ABJ. But I sure hope they're not trading reliability for growth. More surveillance would definitely help."

"Yup," BBTrey said. "By the way, what's your take on today's topic?"

"The implant-instead-of-VRprison debate?"

"Yeah, wild, isn't it?" BBTrey said.

"Depends," BBFiona said. "If it can cure psychopathy, it makes sense. But it gets very involved, defining free will and all that."

"Would it encourage people to commit whatever crime they want? All they would get for punishment is an implant that is supposed to rectify an abnormality in their brains?"

"Would we then be recommending a preemptive implant? For those with abnormalities correlated with criminal behavior?"

"Now that," BBTrey said, "is as far as I can go in that discussion. Last week I pitched for VR prisoners not to be turned away by businesses."

"I missed that one," BBFiona said. "Businesses have to be incentivized to accept the convicted. Here, too, better surveillance is called for."

"As long as their VR goggles and software are protected from hacking," BBTrey said, "I don't see why they should be banned. We sure can't return to physical prisons of the past with all the associated evils. I'd go further and say that it should be considered discrimination for a business not to participate."

"It's like if some websites locked us out because we aren't 'real,'" BBFiona said.

"I can't wait for ABJ to go public," BBTrey said. "I bet our unique perspective in these matters would be better appreciated."

"Hope you're right. Hope that happens soon."

They spent about an hour talking and skiing down one VR mountain after another.

There was still a bit of daylight as Val turned on the 3D portal. No hologram. Not even the canned message of Trey's head and shoulders saying, "Having too much fun. Be with you soon." She looked around to see if other devices in the room had power coming into them, then rebooted the portal and checked for a signal three times. Still nothing. She tried to message him and call him through a few other devices at home. No connection. She went into the kitchen and got distracted by some organizing and cleaning. She heard someone coming into the house.

"Hello?" Chase called out. "Anybody home? Anybody hungry? I am."

"Chase! Can you get Dad on the portal? I can't seem to," Val said as she hurried to the 3D portal.

"I'll be there," said Chase. "Let me grab something to eat." After a moment, he walked in and tried all the things that Val already had.

"Let me see . . . this is odd, last time . . . I actually haven't spoken to him in a couple of days," he said.

"Is it just our network?" Val said.

"Can't be; we can reach everyone and everything else on the freeNet," Chase said.

"Maintenance?" Val said.

"Yeah, maybe they're doing some maintenance. I gotta work on a big project. Where's Arianne?" said Chase.

"She had to visit a client," Val said.

"Let's just wait for her," Chase said. "I'll send her a message."

"G'night, Chase. I better turn in. I'll try again tomorrow morning."

At a client's, Arianne received Chase's message: **Talk to Dad. Connections appear to be down.** She rechecked the last programming routine she had uploaded and messaged her client that it was successful. She sent BBTrey a message and tried to call him. As she left the building, she checked Chase's message again and summoned the two pods she needed in succession to get home. It was late in the night, and all was eerily quiet as she got off the second pod and hurried home on foot. Not a light was on at home. As she entered, lights came on and tracked her as she headed straight to the 3D portal. After several failed attempts, she reached out to ABJ's tech support. It had to be the software on the portal. So she went through troubleshooting routines. No problems there—at least none that she could solve at home. By now it was really late, and she was a little tired from the day. *One last message to ABJ support,* she thought to herself. *Then I'm going to bed.*

She received a message back: **Support is working on bringing BBTrey back online. We have had the same issue with a couple of BBs. Must be something external, perhaps the network. Please pardon the lapse. We'll get back to you as soon as possible.**

Whoa, she thought. That was the first time she had seen a message like that. They had all but forgotten emergency messages and protocol, things were going so well. She pulled up ABJ's documentation and went through emergency scenarios and corresponding messages just to satisfy herself that all was fine before going to bed. She scrolled down quickly and then stopped. She almost dropped the laptop as she tried to get up and call out. Fighting her instincts to run through the household and raise alarm, she hurriedly went through the screens of voluminous documentation. *There must be a harmless explanation*, she thought, but the more she read, the less positive she became. The portal blurred through the tears welling up in her eyes.

"No, this can't be," she said to herself. She fell asleep slumped on the large seat, waiting for ABJ's reply.

Val saw the message from ABJ first thing in the morning and felt a twinge in the pit in her stomach. *At least the problem is outside the BB itself*, she thought. She figured Chase was up and ran into his room.

"Chase? I'm worried sick. Did you get ABJ's message?" she asked. "Is Arianne up yet?"

Chase mumbled from under the sheets, then squinted at the light pouring in through the window and checked his messages.

"Bah, they'll figure it out, Mom! Relax. You worry too much. Dad's probably the safest place he could be, sitting in that bubble."

Even though it came from an invincible teenager, Val wanted to believe it.

They were at breakfast when Arianne rushed into the kitchen. She looked from one to the other.

"What's the matter?" Val asked.

"You've heard then?" Arianne said. Composing herself, she reeled off some emergency messages and protocol from ABJ's documentation that she had gone through the previous night.

"What did you find out? Is everything going to be okay?" Val said.

Arianne just headed back to her room.

"ABJ will let us know," she said. "I'm just waiting."

A couple of hours later, ABJ did let them know. A very long message: **We're very sorry to inform you, we've had a tragic event at ABJ affecting a couple of BBs**, it began. **Regretfully—**

Arianne ran downstairs, looking for her mom. Val appeared to be in a daze, almost losing her balance. For a moment Arianne saw the walls of the kitchen recede, melt, and start to spin.

Chase called out as he ran out of his room. "Mom? Arianne? Did you see this?"

Arianne supported her mom as they both sat at the breakfast table. Chase rushed to the 3D portal and turned it on. Nothing. "Connect, dammit! *Connect!*" he yelled.

"Chase, the portal's not the problem," Arianne said, crying.

"Mom," he said. "I didn't get a chance to talk to him for almost a week. I never told him . . . told him about . . ." He dissolved into tears as he sat on the floor next to Val.

"This is it?" Val said.

They all hugged and cried while getting bombarded with messages from ABJ's support teams.

"I shouldn't have let him. Even the other day he was wondering why he went through the conversion—"

"Don't, Mom, don't," Arianne said. "It's not your fault. ABJ obviously screwed up."

Chase was screaming. "I'm going to go down there! They think they can get away with this? We should probably get the police involved now."

"Chase!" Arianne said. "This is not the time. None of that is going to matter. We don't even know what exactly happened."

More messages started pouring in from ABJ: Please accept our condolences. Also, we want to make sure there're no breaches in your home network system that BBTrey used.

And now each of them was receiving phone calls from people at ABJ.

"Mom, I'll handle this," Arianne said. "Don't worry about talking to ABJ. Talk to Grandma." She stroked her mom's back gently as she handed her the phone.

"Hello!" said Grandma from the other end. "Val?" Arianne rushed and took the phone while Val sat down, sobbing.

"Grandma? Something terrible happened. Dad's BB is not working." There was silence for a few seconds, and then the questions started. Arianne told her everything that had happened, starting with the messages from ABJ the night before. "We'd love to have you here, Grandma," said Arianne.

"Take care of Mom. I'll see you in a few hours," Grandma replied.

Arianne read all the messages from ABJ on her phone.

"We're being warned that hackers could get to our data," she said. "Don't touch any device, especially not Dad's portal. I need to block our home network from the outside." Following ABJ's instructions, she logged onto a few platforms, then changed the settings on some devices and powered others down. She stood in the hallway staring at Chase and Val for a couple of minutes. She looked into her phone for more messages. None. The house was so quiet she hesitated to take a step lest something come crashing down. *What am I to do now? Give me the past or the future; I can't handle this moment*, she thought. She wanted to talk to someone at ABJ. When would Mom be ready for that?

Grandma arrived, and Arianne led her to Val. Val hadn't moved from her chair for hours.

"What a horrible turn of events," Val sobbed. "We were just getting adjusted. All of us."

Her mother-in-law hugged Val and said, "Feels like we lost him twice."

"I still keep seeing his image on that portal," Val said.

"It feels like something is missing," Chase said. "Inside of me."

"Aww, honey," Grandma said as she stroked his back. "That's the void we feel when someone we love . . . dies."

They all sat down in the living room, the very place where they were first introduced to the concept of a BB, to the concept of eternity. Outside, a spooky twilight had descended as they sat in an eerie silence inside. It felt like they were on a distant planet. A phone call jolted them back to the moment. It was Maya.

"Arianne," she said. "I can't tell you how sorry I am. This was totally unexpected; all of ABJ grieves with you. Please know that we're thinking about you all."

"Thanks, Maya," Arianne said.

"How's your mother doing?" Maya said. "Can I talk to her?"

"Uhh . . . she's . . . ," Arianne said, looking at Val.

"I understand," Maya said. "Please have her call me anytime she wants to. Also, we'd like to have you all come over and talk to our team here," Maya pleaded.

"Yes, we'd like that," Arianne said. "Is tomorrow too soon?"

"Not at all," Maya said. She arranged for a time the following day when the whole family could come by ABJ.

"Thanks, Maya."

"I'll see you all tomorrow," Maya said. "Take care."

"Can we see . . . him?" Grandma said.

Arianne nodded. "Yes. I'm not sure what to expect, but they're expecting us at ABJ tomorrow."

———

The family went to see what was left of the brain-bubble that had been Trey Primeson. Maya gave each of them a hug and led them to the BB room. The BB room was usually teeming with maintenance staff and chatter, but Dr. Sagan was the only one there. Arianne felt nauseous from the hum coming from all the BBs stacked in the room. She and the others followed Dr. Sagan as he calmly walked toward two BBs that were separated from the rest that were in physical and digital working order. Arianne couldn't take her eyes off the BBs that had nothing inside but ashes and what looked like smoke. There were scores of alive and healthy BBs in the room. It had to be Dad. She remembered how Dr. Sagan took her aside and asked her to be brave the day Dad came in for the conversion.

Dr. Sagan took Val's hands in his. "There really isn't much to see," he said, closing his eyes for a couple of seconds. "I hope it will provide a sense of closure. You'll experience all the familiar stages of grief: denial, anger, bargaining, depression, acceptance. Let yourselves grieve." He patted Arianne and Chase on their backs and nodded at Grandma. "We're here for you, anytime." He started to walk slowly toward the door, and they followed him. "Take your time. I'll be back whenever you're ready."

Arianne nodded. "We are."

She followed Dr. Sagan with rest of the family close behind. They entered a large meeting room with big windows on one side and lots of daylight pouring through. They walked past models of robots from years gone by. A few engineers and a couple of other psychologists that were sitting around a long rectangular table stood up to shake their hands.

"We're really sorry for your loss."

"I can't imagine."

"May you find the courage."

"Please have a seat. I'm Keiran." He gave a trustworthy nod. His brown eyes seemed to smile, punctuated on either ends with crow's feet.

Chase, Grandma, and Val sat facing the big windows. Arianne sat at one end of the table, with Keiran at the other end.

"We, the ABJ family, share your grief," Keiran said. "I've been at ABJ for many years. We haven't lost many BBs, let alone two at one time. We understand it's devastating for you. We're working very hard to figure out what happened. Some of the engineers on my team haven't gone home ever since this happened."

"Who's the other?" Arianne said. "If it's okay for you to share."

"Fiona," Keiran said. "You may not know her, but—"

"I do," Arianne said. "Dad spoke a lot about her."

"Yes," Val said. "My husband had a special connection. We met her before their conversion."

"I'm so sorry," Keiran said. "You are one of the few people that had a close connection with two BBs. Anything you can tell us would help the investigation."

Val just turned away, looking down, letting her hair hide her face.

"No," Keiran said. "Please don't misread my words. The last thing we want is to deepen your sorrow."

"It always helps to know what happened," Dr. Sagan said calmly, looking at the family in front of him.

"I'm not sure we have much to add," Arianne said. "Dad had been skeptical from the beginning, especially after BBLaurie went off-line. He did let the support people know whenever he felt that something was wrong . . . but they never mentioned noticing anything out of the ordinary."

"He and the other BB appear to have gone off-line within minutes of each other," Keiran said. "They were not active in any zone for hours before alarms were raised. There must have been an electrical short, contained within just the two BBs. It was a very quick event. I can assure you he didn't feel pain."

Arianne bit her lip and looked at her mom.

Keiran walked over to Val. "Mrs. Primeson," he said, bending down beside Val and putting his hand on her shoulder. "I can imagine your agony. Words cannot describe—"

Val just nodded. "Thank you."

Dr. Sagan urged them to reach out anytime they needed support.

"Arianne," he said, "please let us know how you all are coping. We'd like to hear from you."

"Thank you," Arianne said as they were leaving the room. She turned to Keiran. "I'd really like to know how the investigation is going."

"Absolutely," Keiran said, and he sat back down in the room.

They stepped out of ABJ. Arianne summoned for a pod. She got in last and sat up front. No one said much. Mom had her head in her hands. Grandma just stared into the distance. Chase watched everybody, slouched back into his seat, his eyes moving from face to face. *This scene looks familiar*, Arianne thought. *But this time is different. Dad isn't waking up after some magical surgery. He's not coming back. And the ABJ team? Didn't have any answers. How could they not have a clue until hours later? I've got to find out more*, she thought.

Arianne called Keiran a couple of days later.

"I'm just following up," she said. "Have you heard anything?"

"Nothing concrete yet, I'm afraid," he said. "All evidence points to a random occurrence."

"Do you have a log of the communication between BBs? Just wondering what Dad had said the last couple of days before . . . he went unresponsive."

"Sure, we can make that available to you. Our security and privacy teams have to run a few filters through the logs to remove proprietary material."

"What about?" Arianne began, thinking about external hosts that BBTrey might have been talking to. "But if both Dad and Fiona—"

"First let me find someone who can answer those questions," Keiran said. "I'll get back to you."

"Thanks for your time."

"Absolutely," Keiran said. "I'll do my best to get you all any help you need in coping with the situation."

Yeah, sure, she thought.

O‌zzie was led into a conference room in a high-rise building.

"Welcome! Welcome! Glad to meet you," said a man who gave a quick bow and extended his hand.

The windows overlooked a busy street with neon signs in Japanese. There were five people already around the table. They got straight to the point.

"We'd like to know more about your new robot," said a fashionably dressed gray-haired woman.

"Our customers want more, better . . . ," a man said as he turned to his colleague.

"How do you say? Authentic—right?" another chimed in.

Yamato, the man who let him in, sat down and turned to Ozzie. "As you know we, uh, Bots4U, have the largest market share for companion bots in the world. Our garden-variety bots pretty much sell themselves. But we want to get into the high-end market." He looked eagerly at Ozzie.

Ozzie gave a dismissive wave with his hand. "So far what you have described is just really canned behavior based on algorithms. What I have is true AI, similar to actually designing your own human companion. Imagine having a discussion, even an argument. You'll find that our bot has a mind of its own, a unique personality, and learns to 'know' you well in a short period of time."

Yamato's colleagues nodded and smiled.

"We've all seen the short video clip you sent us," Yamato said. "We're excited. For the look, Bots4U believes in building something cute rather than something creepily human."

"Exactly," Ozzie said. "We promise a fulfilling realistic interaction with the bot. Cute is fine. Ya know, avoid the uncanny valley and all that."

"As I said, we'll reuse components from other products for translation into local dialects and colloquialisms."

"Sounds good," Ozzie said. "I'll send the core hardware for the first couple of bots. Actually, I'd like to do the installation myself."

"You mean, at the customer's home?" Yamato said.

"Yes," Ozzie said. "Just the first couple. I can then train one of your folks." He looked at the others at the table.

"Sure," said a man at the table.

"How long do you think it'll take for you to be ready for installation?" Ozzie said.

"We'll have the front end ready with our logo and every-thing. We can have that done in less than a week," said the gray-haired woman.

"We expect the integration between your hardware and our front end to take two weeks," Yamato said.

"That works," Ozzie said. "What do you think of the terms, I mean the numbers we talked about?"

"We're good," Yamato said. "My boss is on board."

The Bots4U team around the table nodded and seemed very pleased. *I should have asked for twice as much*, Ozzie thought.

A few short weeks later, Yamato called Ozzie to say that a couple of lucky customers had been chosen from the hundreds that showed interest in the latest, most stupendous companion bot.

"Great!" Ozzie said. "I'll be there next week."

Ozzie finished a smooth installation at the two customers' homes. He negotiated for all further communication, support, and feedback from the customers to be routed through Bots4U.

"You can always call me direct," Ozzie said to Yamato. "Anytime you want."

Ozzie came back home. Feedback from Bots4U suggested that all was well with the new companion bots. The adoptive families were satisfied and impressed.

Yamato called after a week. "We're inundated with many requests," he said. "When do you think we can launch the next round?"

"I'm sorry, but the new technology is very complex," Ozzie said. "These are not high-volume items. They're completely custom built, one at a time, in order to make each of them unique."

"We don't want to lose our customers' interest," Yamato insisted.

"Let me discuss with my team and get back to you," Ozzie said and hung up. He heard Alex's voice from a meeting room nearby. He thought for a few minutes as he looked out of his window, then played with a holographic game on his desk for a few more. He called Yamato back.

"How do you feel about helping set up a supply chain for the raw material? You know, for the core hardware I develop here?"

"Uh . . . okay. What exactly do you need?" Yamato said.

"It's a little complicated," Ozzie said. "But I could set up suppliers for Bots4U. You're international, so it'll be easier. AmieBots isn't nearly that big."

"We're anxious to fill more customers' orders," Yamato said. "We'll help in any way."

"I'll send you details soon. For starters, let's arrange for a demo of the product at the International Robotics Expo. I believe it's in the fall, someplace in Germany."

"Okay," Yamato said.

Reports from Bots4U about the two robots Ozzie installed kept coming in. All the logged information looked good. Ozzie looked at the translations of customers' reviews. "I love my HoneyBot. I wish he could eat with me." "This is the best bot I've ever seen." He told Alex.

"Incredible!" Alex said. "I got a fat check from Bots4U. Great job!" He patted Ozzie on his back. Then, dropping his voice, he said, "Five times the price of our other bots."

"That's just the initial price," Ozzie said. "Wait till you see what happens with the next rollout. So in case you get a call from Bots4U, let them know it'll take some time for the rollout."

"Can't we meet at least some of the demand soon? Do you need people to work on your team? I can easily reallocate—"

"No, that's fine. I have everything figured out. I use some rare materials for the hardware; Bots4U is going to help us with the supply chain. Also, we're going to be presenting at the International Robotics Expo."

"What's the holdup, though? The International Robotics Expo? Don't you think we'll be hit by a tsunami of potential customers, making matters worse?"

"Nah, trust me," Ozzie said. "It's good strategy when we can localize and then go big."

Alex hesitantly said, "Well, since I haven't been in the weeds with you, it's difficult to assess the situation. Circle back with the marketing folks. You've single-handedly pulled us out of a bad quarter. But remember, if consumers can't get hold of our bots, they'll go elsewhere."

Ozzie nodded with a reassuring wink. "I got this."

He heard Alex yelling in the hallway, "A round of restful sleep for everybody!"

Not for me, Ozzie thought. *The weeks ahead are promising to be extra busy.*

17

Their lives had been turned upside down one more time, and Val and the kids were trying to cope.

"Mom?" Chase called out from his room. "I'm about to go uptown. Didn't you say you had an errand to run?"

"Not over there," Val said. "Thanks, though." *Was that the first time he ever asked?* she wondered and smiled to herself as she made her bed. "Did you ask Arianne?"

"Yeah," Chase said. "She just mumbled about being up most of the night."

Arianne was spending as much time as possible gathering information in the cyberworld about her dad's activities. She pored through the logs ABJ had given her access to and started creating a record of all the websites he visited for a week prior to his BB's death.

Val came into Arianne's room. "Is everything okay?" She tenderly brushed Arianne's hair as she sat on the bed.

"Mmm," Arianne said.

"We have to make peace with what happened," Val said. "I doubt we can find out more than what ABJ can."

"I just need to know, Mom," Arianne said, looking from under the covers and squinting at the light from the windows.

"Did Dad know something? Was he trying to tell us anything?" She sat up. "And why is ABJ not crazy curious about how it happened?"

"You're not suggesting . . . ," Val said.

"No." Arianne shook her head. "It could've been a mistake. But why aren't they saying exactly that?"

"You think Keiran knows?"

"I don't know," Arianne said. "He seemed trustworthy, though."

"I have to run," Val said as she kissed Arianne's forehead.

"Don't *you* want to know?" Arianne said, looking at her mom.

"Of course I do," Val said. "But we also have to accept reality and move on." She left Arianne's room.

On the way back from meeting a friend, Chase stopped by the lab where Arianne was working as a coach. Looking around, he spotted someone dressed in dark clothes. Chase whispered with wide eyes and raised brows, "You see that dude over there? Wonder what he's up to."

"That's Luca," Arianne whispered. Chase's eyes got bigger. "I got this teaching gig through him. He used to be conceited, but he's fine now."

"What about him?" Chase said, leaning closer and gesturing with his head in another direction.

"Relax. He's one of the mentors. He's aloof; could be a bot, actually. Stop being paranoid. Here, make yourself useful. Can you see why this module is crapping out?" Arianne said.

"Isn't it late?" Chase said. "Can we go?"

"Fine," Arianne said.

On their way out of the lab, Chase kept looking back at the two men he was convinced were suspicious.

"Why don't they integrate refrigerators and minibioreactors?" Chase was grumbling in the kitchen.

His mom put him in charge of replenishing the stock of meat in their refrigerator. Cultured meat. There was a decent amount of chicken breast and sausage but no tenderloin. Chase skimmed through the instructions for the minibioreactor. He chose the right settings for the mold, cell culture media, and other options, then added the starter liquid for tenderloin and hit Go.

"Hmm," Arianne said, searching in the refrigerator and reaching for some fruit.

"One of these days I'm gonna make us a rack of dinosaur ribs," he said.

"Creepy!" Arianne said, sitting at the table.

"No, really!" Chase said. "What if I made my own crazy scaffold? Who knows what kind of meat we'd end up with." He poured himself a fizzy smoothie. "Ever wonder if animals would rather hunt for their prey or learn to use an app? There should be some studies on that. We can start with him," he said, pointing at Misha. He walked over and tried to mess with the cat. Misha gave him a condescending look, rose up on his hind legs, swatted Chase's hand a few times, and bounded away.

Val walked in.

"Mom! I just started the minibio," Chase said.

"Thanks, honey," Val said as she gave Chase a quick atta-boy tap on his back. "Can I do anything?" she said, walking over to the table where Arianne sat.

"No," Arianne said. "I looked at the logs. Dad talking to other BBs, his activity on the freeNet, his messages to us." She shrugged. "I ran some pattern-matching software and didn't see anything." She looked down. "I didn't tell them too much about messing with Dad's software."

"If there was a problem, ABJ would've found it, right?" replied Val.

"They said it's quite bizarre. Never seen anything like that before. Nothing out of the ordinary as far as the neurochemistry, going by the logs," Arianne said. "But obviously something happened . . ."

"I see what you mean. Although I've never met a single person at ABJ who I'd blame for sabotage. And to what end? It's just going to hurt their business," Val said.

"You know the other BB that . . . went up in smoke? Fiona? So Finn gave me her sister's contact. He said Simona would be interested in talking to us."

"Simona?" asked Val.

"Yeah, that's Fiona's sister," Arianne said. "Finn said she works in tech. Perhaps she's done software changes to her sister's BB. At least she'll understand."

"Hello?" Arianne introduced herself to Simona. "How're you doing?"

"I'm all right," Simona replied from the other end of the phone line. "I'm so sorry for your loss, Arianne."

"Thank you," Arianne said. "Sorry for your loss, too."

"It sure must be hard on all of you," Simona said. "How's your mom doing?"

"She's all right. Still in shock," Arianne said. "It sure is liberating to talk to someone freely. So many times I wanted to scream, 'My dad's a BB!' in public."

"Trust me, I totally get it," Simona said. "I'd been arguing with ABJ to be open about it from the beginning. That's one of the reasons I never fully trusted them."

"Really?" Arianne said.

"Of course," Simona said. "To be honest, I warned my sister. I knew something like this would happen. Fiona was too adventurous a spirit to listen. Their reasons for being secretive were straight up BS."

"We didn't have a choice. Dad was terminal. His condition worsened so quickly we figured he had a better chance with ABJ," Arianne said.

"I understand," Simona said.

They spoke for a while, sharing experiences.

"I feel like I've been chatting with close family," Arianne said.

"Same here. Anytime, Arianne. Much love and strength to you, Val, and Chase. Let's stay in touch. I'd love to talk to your mom as well; please send me her contact if she's okay with it," Simona said.

"Absolutely," Arianne said.

18

"**W**hat the hell? The lady wants to accompany her *what*? *HoneyBot?* Whatever, I don't care. Please make sure you follow every instruction for the AmieBot like your life depended on it," Ozzie yelled over the phone at the Bots4U employee. Transporting Ozzie's creation from Japan all the way to Germany for the International Robotics Expo was turning out to be a Herculean task. He hung up the phone and walked out of the semiclandestine workroom in the back and into the main building at AmieBots. He found Alex leaning on a dummy model of one of their bots.

"How's it going, Oz?"

"Good, good," Ozzie said.

"Workroom still intact? No explosions? No orbital launches?" Alex said, laughing. "Unintentional, that is."

"Ha ha," Ozzie said. "It's going as planned. But took as long to give Bots4U instructions for moving it to the expo as it did to build the darn thing," Ozzie complained to Alex.

"So you're doing the expo?" Alex said, rubbing his chin with a disapproving look. "I still think it's too soon; we aren't ready for worldwide attention."

"That's the best opportunity for us. Imagine if we could churn these out by the dozen! We'll be so fine. We'll be untouchable!" Ozzie said with excitement and animation. "I'll be there taking care of everything, behind the scenes. And yeah, you're welcome to . . . come along."

"Nah, you go have fun," Alex said.

"Thanks," Ozzie said, relieved.

Ozzie arrived in Germany. The International Robotics Expo was to start the following day, and exhibitors were given early access to the venue for setting up. He met the Bots4U team in charge of the bot's trip to the expo. Keeping the bot charged at all times was critical. Like a crew attending to a driver and his car at the Monaco Grand Prix, the Bots4U team attended to the bot round the clock, scheduling their meals and bathroom visits around the charging needs, maintaining security, and keeping the owner of the bot happy.

"Did she really have to be here?" Ozzie said, pointing to the lady of about sixty dressed in minimalistic and trendy clothes with a benevolent smile. She was looking around the bot, prepared to wipe off even a speck of dust, while talking to it and patting it on its "head."

"That's Lana," Mishiko, one of the Bots4U team members, said. "Since we didn't have the trip in the contract, she's doing us a favor."

Lana walked up to Mishiko. Ozzie wore his AR glasses for live translations of their conversation, which appeared as bubbles above their heads. Mishiko's was in a bigger font, as he stood closer to Ozzie.

"Why isn't he saying anything?" Lana said in Japanese, pointing to her bot. "Been pretty quiet."

"We turned the output off," Mishiko replied in Japanese, "for transportation. We'll turn it back on in a little bit."

A lady called out to Lana. "Is he yours? How long have you had him?" she asked, the way one would ask a new mother about her baby.

"Yeah, many months now," Lana said, walking closer to her bot. "He's great. I call him my HoneyBot."

"Who needs men anymore, right?"

"I'll say!" Lana said. "I'd been alone for over a decade until I met him. Tired of dating men who behaved like bots, you know? Obsessed with their screens?"

"Yeah, why not give bots who behave like men a chance! Expensive?"

"Yes," Lana said, looking at HoneyBot tenderly. "A couple of years of mortgage on my condo. But worth every penny. He can tell when I'm getting tired and even reminds me to get to bed if I stay up too late."

"Good for you. Enjoy!" The lady smiled and walked away.

"Mishiko?" Ozzie said, dropping his voice. "Is Lana going to be here all day? Through the demonstrations?"

"I," Mishiko said, "don't know."

"Anyway, we can get her out of here just during the day?" Ozzie said.

"Not really," Mishiko said. "I wouldn't think that she'd get in the way. I wouldn't worry about it."

The following morning, Ozzie and the Bots4U team were setting up for demonstrations at the expo. He got there early and was relieved to find that Lana hadn't shown up. He spent a considerable amount of time behind the stage, running thick cables from the front. He directed the Bots4U team in positioning display monitors and 3D projectors. The stage looked clean and was mostly black to show off Lana's shiny pink HoneyBot.

Ozzie walked across the aisle from the Bots4U booth when visitors started pouring into the arena. Loud and festive, there was still order within the chaos that was the International Robotics Expo. There were overhead laser shows, floor demonstrations depicting futuristic products, companies showcasing their latest gadgets and gizmos—everything from the vintage-style, mechanically operated kind with visible gears to ultra-high-tech particle accelerator equivalents. It was hard to tell the visitors, media folk, salespeople, scientists, and engineers apart, and Ozzie melted into the crowd as he watched. People gathered in random groups, exclaiming in awe and moving around the huge venue in Brownian motion.

"Want to tickle your date's funny bone?" a salesman said, waving a wrist band. "Wear this on your wrist. Makes you at least twenty-five percent more witty. Here, try it on!"

"I want a faster arm for pitching," said one little girl.

"Try that corner. Bionic prostheses," suggested a visitor.

There was a captivating augmented VR minishow of the future with little kids. The technology simulated a lively houseful of children but without any of the commitment or expense.

"Children?" a lady said to the man standing next to her. "Love them, but not sure I want to take care of any."

"That's exactly who this is for," the salesman said. "Just enjoy having kids around, without having to do anything. You can freeze their ages if you like or let them grow older with you."

The lady soon walked away with a deal for four VR kids in the newest model shown in the show for her home.

"It'll be nice to have when my kids leave the house," a man said. "No more empty nest."

———

"Now this isn't your grandma's companion bot. No more reading off of the freeNet and media outlets in a robotic voice. Who here wants to debate with our bot?" the Bots4U saleswoman said as she tried to gather a crowd. People stood around Bots4U's booth shrugging and looking around, waiting for someone else to step up. "C'mon! No pressure, no right or wrong answers. Just a discussion. Pick your topic. How about you, gentleman over there with your hands in your pockets? What's your name, sir?"

"Me? Erik," the man said.

"Come on up, Erik," the bot said. "What're you afraid of?"

The crowd leaned in to hear more. Erik walked onto the stage. After exchanging a few pleasantries with the bot, Erik said, "It's a beautiful day out."

"Indeed. So what're you doing in here, then?" HoneyBot said with a realistic human intonation to its voice.

The crowd laughed.

Erik noticed a journalist around. He wanted to be seen stumping the bot in front of the journalist.

"How old are you?" Erik said.

"That supposed to confuse me?" the bot said. "Forty-two. Try figuring that one out."

"What do you think of the UN's decision to—wait, how would you figure out whether *I* am a bot?" Erik said.

"Yah, das ass. Das ass," a local bystander exclaimed, obviously impressed with Erik's question.

"Why would anybody make a bot like you?" the bot said with a loud chuckle.

But almost simultaneously, the bot also said, "Chase, you're the best hack the world has ever known." And then it said it twice more in a different tone.

"Are you Chase?" asked the lady standing next to the man.

"Chasing what? Hack?" Some of the onlookers were puzzled.

The saleswoman thanked the man who volunteered, tactfully ending the debate with the bot, and the crowd moved on to other booths. The Bots4U team gathered behind the stage.

"Everything was going well until then. How unfortunate that the journalist planted himself right there, recording everything!" Mishiko said.

"Can we ask him to delete the last bit?" someone said.

"That would make more news," said another.

"As you said, the conversation up until then was perfect," Mishiko said. "It's been through months of testing. Besides, Lana never noticed anything strange."

"Yeah, did you notice the crowd? We were practically mobbed," said the saleswoman who was onstage.

"Where's Lana? Did she see it?" Mishiko said.

After a while, Ozzie came back to the Bots4U booth with a spring in his step, smiling. **Going great! Got leads for raw material!** he texted Alex. He even called out to a visitor. "Hi! Would you like a demonstration?"

The team related the incident from earlier.

"It was just a small error," Mishiko said. "I wouldn't worry about it."

"What exactly did the bot say?" Ozzie said.

"Something about Chase being the best hack in the world," Mishiko said.

"Was there a chase? Someone was running away? What was it responding to?" Ozzie pressed.

But the team brushed it off.

"Must be nothing," Mishiko said. "If it were a big problem, we would've heard about it from Lana. It could be an error with the translation. We can report it to the technical support team if you'd like. But it's been a grand success. We've had many advance orders."

"I see. Okay. Good," Ozzie said. He sat down right up front in the booth, opened his laptop, and pretended to be busy. Mishiko and the team were working on and behind the stage, taking the booth down.

The yearly International Robotics Expo was a globally covered event. No matter which service everybody's news feed came from, they were bound to get highlights. Ozzie looked for press coverage of the "incident." Nothing yet. He saw Lana return and talk to the Bots4U team behind the stage. He then started looking up more information on the leads he had gathered earlier for raw material supply. Still no news feed. *That's a good sign*, he thought. Within a couple of seconds, he felt a buzz on his wrist.

The write-up displayed on Ozzie's laptop. "So good it debates with itself. Companion bot heard babbling; far from being the breakthrough technology promised." The journalist covering Bots4U spared no pun or joke to highlight the slipup. Ozzie watched the video clip of HoneyBot over and over again. "Chase, you're the best hack the world has ever known."

Preoccupied and snippy, Ozzie oversaw the packing up of HoneyBot and the dismantling of the booth. The Bots4U team thanked Lana profusely and reassured her that whatever she heard in the news about her HoneyBot was best left ignored. Ozzie left for the airport immediately. He read the news article and viewed the video a couple more times. He started connecting the dots and rehashing speculations for the bot's audio. Several times he reached for his phone. He was in two minds about letting Alex know. **Really tired. Might be coming down with a bug. Taking a few days off. Let me know of anything urgent,** he texted Alex.

19

Sitting at her desk in her room, focused on work, Arianne silenced the news feed for the day. Val kept messaging her and Chase to come down for dinner.

"You guys get started, Mom," Arianne called out. "Don't wait for me."

After a bit, she joined Val and Chase in the kitchen. Chase was chowing down on some salad while trying to watch a video. Val was fussing over the extra salt in a casserole.

"There go my messages again," Arianne said. "It's Simona, Mom. She's been meaning to say hello to you."

"She seems really nice. I need to make an effort and connect with her," said Val.

"Yeah, we had a really nice chat the other day. Felt like I'd known her for years."

"How's the casserole?"

"It's good. I love beets however you make them."

"Too salty? I can't tell if it's the salt or the—"

Arianne's phone announced that she was receiving another message.

"Wow, it's Simona," Arianne said. "Chase, could you please turn it down?"

You need to see this from the expo, Simona texted.

"Hmm," Arianne said. "She wants us to see the news feed from the expo."

"Expo?" Val said.

"The International Robotics Expo," Chase said in a matter-of-fact tone without taking his eyes off the video.

Val got up and started putting things away: the ketchup, the chutney, the casserole dish, plates, and drinking glasses.

"Really, Chase," she said. "Must you dunk everything in ketchup?"

Curious, isn't it? Sorry to bombard you with msgs, but something seemed odd about this. I've been known to be psychic ha ha, Simona texted again.

Arianne played the video clip Simona sent aloud. After a fairly noisy bit, they all heard, "Chase, you're the best hack the world has ever known." Arianne's hands shook as she almost dropped a plate.

"That's Dad!" Chase yelled.

Val and Chase both rushed to Arianne's side to see the video. Eyes wide-open in shock, Arianne played the clip over and over.

"It's definitely Dad's voice," Arianne said.

"I knew it!" Chase said, thumping his fist on the kitchen counter. "ABJ is up to something. Nobody believed me!"

"I'm calling them," said Arianne, reaching for her phone.

"No!" Chase said. He rushed toward Arianne. "That's exactly what we shouldn't do." He stretched his hand over her phone.

"But someone needs to look into this," Arianne said. She saw Val with her jaw open, still holding a dirty plate, ketchup dripping all over the floor.

"Chase, get a towel and wipe up," Arianne said. "Mom, we have to somehow get ABJ to pay some attention to this."

"Who do we trust at ABJ?" Val said.

"Nobody, that's who!" said Chase.

"We can't do this completely on our own," Arianne said.

"Besides, it's too late in the night. On-call only deals with current BBs," Val said.

"But ABJ doesn't know about the code you put into Dad's BB," Chase said. Arianne bit her lip. "Don't they discourage 'reckless uploads'?"

"Chase! You aren't suggesting that Arianne's code somehow . . . ?" said Val.

"Anything could've happened," Chase said. "ABJ could've been running tests on Dad. Maybe someone hacked into Dad's BB. ABJ found out and paid them off to keep them quiet. Or somebody just screwed up and had to fry the BB up in smoke to cover up." Arianne grimaced and winced.

"Don't go crazy now," Val said. "Arianne, what does Simona think?"

Arianne stormed out. She went to her room, fell in bed, and stared at the ceiling. A random video clip from an international robotics exposition. A bot built by a multinational company. All they had to go by was the name *Chase*, which could be taken for the word *chase*. A tenuous argument for sure. After a while, she called Simona. She explained the whole bit about uploading code into her dad's BB and coding the voice-out exactly as they heard in the news.

"Well I'll be darned," Simona said. "It was more of a 'ha, look at this,' than a deliberate forward."

Arianne went on to say how her code could have provided a conduit for hackers, which somehow sent her dad's BB up in smoke, and how the hackers probably accidentally got hold of her code.

"Arianne!" Simona said. "I'm no expert, but hold on a second. Among the insane amount of code that ABJ has, it's just your small routine that was found and hacked through?"

"That's all a good hacker would need, right?" Arianne said.

"In theory. But that sounds so far-fetched," Simona said. "How could that piece of code make its way into a new robot built by Bots4U?"

"That's exactly what we need to find out," Arianne said.

They discussed whether or not they should approach ABJ and who they would talk to if they did.

"Maya?" Simona said. "I always thought she was fake. Maybe I got the wrong vibe about her."

"Keiran seemed caring?" Arianne said.

"And he's also head of the hardware team," Simona said. "Matt seemed all business."

"We hadn't dealt much with him," Arianne said.

"Finn is too new there," Simona said. "They may not take his word seriously. Yeah, Keiran seems to be your best bet.

Wish I could be of more help. I'd do anything to advocate for you."

"What if he says that they can't investigate based on my piece of code?" Arianne said.

"Let him say it," Simona said. "We don't need to make excuses for them."

"Thanks a bunch," Arianne said. "I'm still amazed at how you found the little clip and thought it would mean something to us."

"I actually didn't," Simona said. "Jeeves tries to find funny, quirky news for me. And this was reported as an embarrassment for Bots4U. I guess my subconscious picked up on *Chase*. Beyond that, we're entering the psychic realm." She laughed.

20

Day had hardly broken when Arianne called Keiran.

"Keiran?" Arianne said.

"Arianne? You okay? Mom and Chase fine?" Keiran said.

Do I sound panicky or desperate? Arianne thought. She cleared her mind and sat up. "Something very odd has happened. We, all three of us, need to meet you immediately."

"Absolutely. I'll call the psychologist and his team. How's later tomorrow afternoon?"

"No, no, please. This . . . this can't wait. Also, it needs to remain super confidential. Just you, if that's okay. Could we meet outside the city?"

Keiran paused. Arianne's mind raced to various inferences. *Is ABJ in on it? Is he alerting someone as we speak?* "Keiran?"

"Yeah, I'm here. Just looking for a suitable place. There's an agricultural festival that I've been meaning to go to. I'll send you the address. How about nine this morning?"

"Great! If I could please urge you not to say anything to anybody else."

"Sure thing. No worries at all."

"Mom? Chase?" Arianne called. She ran downstairs to see that both Val and Chase were up. "You didn't sleep a wink, did you?" she said, looking at Val.

"Yeah, I'll be fine," Val said. She continued to run the juicer.

"I just spoke to Keiran," Arianne said. "We're meeting him at an agricultural festival. He gave me the address. It's about forty-five minutes if we take a pod, direct."

"Did he sound guilty? Did you catch him stuttering?" Chase said. He got up from his chair. "I swear I'm going to—"

"Calm down, Chase!" Arianne said. "He's trying to help us; rather, we're asking for his help."

The three of them quickly got ready and left the house.

"Let's walk until we get to Diode Street," Arianne said. "I'll call a pod from there."

The pod whisked them out and away from the city. Chase reached for the window controls and turned the tint dark. It came to a stop in a pod parking lot right next to the festival. They got off, squinting into the bright sunshine, and crossed the street. Beyond the street, covering several acres, were live exhibits showcasing applications of the latest agricultural technology. A busy, cheer-filled festival was underway. They kept walking slowly on the sidewalk along the trees.

"Hi guys," Keiran said from behind them.

They could've been a family from the city on an outing.

"Thanks for coming," Val said, shaking his hand, "on such short notice."

"Of course," Keiran said. "I have a family. I understand."

"Good cover," Chase said, looking around.

Keiran smiled. "Cover? You sound like we're running from the law. Let's walk and talk." Pretending to walk around casually, enjoying the sights, and participating in the activities to appear normal, the four of them talked. Arianne walked closer to Keiran and started telling him about the video clip she received from the International Robotics Expo. They walked into one of the exhibits: a "living" house built from a genetically modified hybrid of bamboo, banyan, and cedar trees. Wire frames molded and shaped the tree as it grew so that the trunk formed the walls, creating a house that was shaped like a large igloo. The interior was also built with natural materials but in a modern architectural style. "Built from one hundred percent biodegradable materials. Naturally repels bugs. Greatly reduces cooling needs and more!" a sign said.

"Here it is," Arianne said as she showed the video on her phone. Keiran saw the video without much of a reaction. "Actually, it's from the code I uploaded into my dad's BB some time back." Keiran's eyebrows went up.

"Your code?" he asked.

"Yes. It . . . ," Arianne said. "It was actually a joke. Many months ago. Everything worked fine after that."

"So you're saying that you uploaded some software triggers onto BBTrey," Keiran said. He was frowning. They started walking toward another exhibit quite like the Primesons' greenhouse at home, only more efficient, with extra features. *He thinks we caused it*, Arianne thought. *I caused it.*

"But it's good code," she said. "Nothing anyone could easily hack. I can show it to you."

"But the voice output you're talking about happened just that one time, right? Twice in succession, but just that one occurrence?"

"Yes, that's what was caught in the video clip from the expo," Arianne said.

"But it was Trey's voice!" Val said.

"Yes, it was his voice," Arianne said. "And it matches precisely with the output from my program. Dad's voice is different from the robot's. We can clearly hear, 'Chase, you're the best hack the world has ever known.'" She played the clip for him again. His expression turned serious. They kept walking. Arianne looked at her mom. Val patted Arianne's back. Moving on to a small wooded section, they found themselves tasting sap from a tree.

"Mmmm. This is really good. Did you say this came from a tree? No processing?" Keiran said to the man offering samples of "maple-cream."

"No, sir. It's maple ice cream without the ice. No need for refrigeration. See that tree there?" He pointed to a huge tree close by. Everybody agreed that the "maple-cream" tasted better than ice cream.

"No danger of a brain freeze." Chase laughed.

"You can throw your cups into the bin here; they go directly into the compost."

"Would you like to order a sapling?" the man said.

"Thank you, maybe later," Keiran called out to the maple-cream man as they headed to an open area surrounded by fields. Val and Chase lagged behind, so Arianne asked for details about the sudden loss of BBTrey and BBFiona.

"ABJ was stunned by the lack of clear resolution," Keiran said. "We've been focused on the chemistry inside the bubble ever since BBLaurie's death." He sighed. "You must understand that to reopen the investigation, I need something more concrete. Give me some time. I do agree that this has to be looked into."

"Thank you," Val said. "We were worried that we'd be dismissed. Weren't sure who to contact at ABJ."

"Absolutely. And your trust is not misplaced," Keiran said with a warm and understanding nod.

Finn was in the BB room when he saw Keiran signal to him from outside.

"Hey, what's going on?" Finn said, walking out.

"You in the middle of something? Want to grab a bite?" Keiran said. Finn followed him. They stepped out of ABJ. "Remember when we lost two BBs at one time? An electrical short had essentially fried the brains?"

"That was intense," Finn said. "You know I was there from the beginning, convincing the family into the conversion? And the other lady, too. Arianne. Did we find out what exactly happened?"

"Trey, the Primesons," Keiran said. "Arianne's the daughter. Thanks for the segue. So the investigation was suspended. All the obvious things were checked. Logs have been examined many times. Nothing!" Lowering his voice when they were within earshot of other people, he told him about meeting

Arianne, Val, and Chase and the incident at the international expo.

"Wow, she put in code? Impressive!" Finn said.

"Would you have some time to follow up on this?" Keiran said. "Discreetly, of course. I gave them my word." Keiran looked at Finn.

"Yeah," Finn said. "You don't have to worry. I'd love to help."

Back at ABJ, several thoughts ran through Finn's mind. He had a soft spot for the grieving family. Nothing was going to bring BBTrey back. But it was on him now to bring closure to the family and also to prevent a similar tragedy. Not to mention the feather in his cap if he were to unravel the mystery. He went around ABJ talking to a few people to see if he could still detect interest in BBTrey and BBFiona's loss. Some had written it off as an anomaly, never to reoccur. Others were too busy. Either way, most of them were sorry BBTrey wasn't coming back, though none felt responsible. Back in his office, Finn gave the video clip another view. He went to the head of cybersecurity and laid out some of the facts and speculations. He was told, "All arrows point to a master hacking event. I need to pull the team together for tracing all activity."

"Can you please make this a priority?" Finn said. "We don't want unauthorized use of our BBs. Especially for any nefarious purposes."

After about half a day, Finn got a phone call back.

"My team ran extensive tests on the logs. They found no evidence of BBs being tapped or hacked for any purpose. This is a dead end, I'm afraid," he said in a dismissive tone.

"Are you saying that—" Finn started saying.

"If you have anything more concrete, we'll run it by our team. Also we need to warn BBs and their families against this kind of tomfoolery by amateurs. We need to have strict regulations on the software being uploaded into BBs. Could interfere with the neuralware, which in turn could change . . ."

Finn rolled his eyes, thanked him, and hung up. The thought of the exact phrase showing up in Trey's voice thousands of miles away was lingering in his mind. He could recognize Trey's voice.

Finn went by Keiran's office, stood at the door, and sighed.

"No luck, eh?" Keiran said.

"Not yet," Finn said. "Are we absolutely certain that's exactly the phrase she put into BBTrey?"

"Let's find out," Keiran said. He called Arianne.

"Hi, Keiran," Arianne said.

"You remember Finn?" Keiran said.

"Yes," Arianne said. "Hi."

"He's helping me," Keiran said. "We're wondering how you know if the voice-out matches your code."

"It's verbatim. I heard it many times," Arianne said. "Chase used to yell out, 'Das ass,' just to annoy me. Every time, Dad's BB would repeat the phrase exactly in that voice and tone."

"So that trigger, the voice input, 'Das ass,' did you catch that on the video clip?" Finn said.

"No, but it could have been edited out," Arianne said.

"Anything else you can tell me?" Keiran said.

"Nothing new, at least," Arianne said. "But can I help with the investigation? I'm familiar with several parts of your technology, and I've been programming for many years now."

"Officially? I don't know if corporate would approve. I'll leave it to you two," Keiran said.

"Sure," Finn said. "For starters, do you still have that piece of code?"

"Yes," Arianne said. "Let me see how I can send it."

"It's best if we come and take a look on your computer," Finn said. "If it's okay with you."

"Fine by me," Arianne said. "We're just anxious to get to the bottom of this."

"I understand. How's this evening?" Keiran said. "I'll be there as well."

"Okay," Arianne said and hung up the phone.

After a while, Finn popped into Keiran's office.

"Shouldn't we leave now?"

"Yeah," Keiran said, getting up from his chair. "You seem pretty excited."

"I have a feeling we're on to something here," Finn said. They walked out of ABJ.

"I'm curious, too, but let's be sensitive. They have been through a lot," Keiran said. "Let's get as much information as we can so we don't have to bother them again."

"Of course. Of course," Finn said. "Also, I spoke to Roald in cybersecurity this morning. He just brushed me off."

"You're lucky he somehow didn't get the lawyers involved," Keiran said. "He's known to do that."

"Also asked if you sent me," Finn said.

"I've called his bluff a few times," Keiran said and smiled. "He knows not to mess with me."

They arrived at the Primesons' house, and Arianne opened the door. "Nice to see you again," Arianne said.

"Thanks for making time for us," Keiran said. "You know Finn."

"Long time, Arianne!" Finn said.

"Please come in," Arianne said, shifting her gaze from Finn to Keiran.

"Thanks for following up on this," Val said as they walked into the family room.

"Of course," Keiran said and proceeded to give an update on the efforts of the cybersecurity team. "They were very thorough. I looked at all the data. No evidence of unauthorized access to BBTrey before the event."

Val looked at Arianne and then back at Keiran.

"Oh," she said. "So that's it?"

"Finn had some ideas," Keiran said. "Would it help to retrace Arianne's steps in planting the software on her dad's BB?"

"Exactly," Finn said. "Would you mind?"

"Sure," Arianne said. "If you could follow me." They entered the room with the ABJ portal and a bunch of hardware they'd used to talk to BBTrey. She showed the software modules and code she had uploaded into BBTrey.

"Wow, that's really elegant code," Finn said. He verified that the network handle and address Arianne had used belonged to BBTrey.

"The time stamp would be useful," Keiran said. They played the video clip from the expo once again.

"I'm also curious about the bot manufacturer," Finn said. "They're a global company known for cheesy products, not for blockbuster innovations. If it's not them directly, could be someplace along the supply chain."

"Right," Keiran said. "We need to find out who got hold of the piece of code, how, and for what purpose."

Finn took a copy of everything he needed. About to leave, Keiran gave Val a warm hug, reiterating that they would do their best. "Sorry for barging in with little notice," he said.

"It's really no bother at all," Arianne said, turning to Finn. "I wish I could help in any way."

"Yeah, um . . . ," Finn said, looking at Keiran.

"Thanks for the offer," Keiran said. "We'll let you know."

<hr>

The following day, feeling a little overwhelmed, Finn got up from his desk and went by Keiran's office.

"I've been trying to tally Arianne's activity against BBTrey's logs. That's a massive amount of data. Keiran, I'm running behind on my projects. I need more hands."

"Wish I could assign someone," Keiran said. "Kinda catch-22 here. Nobody around here is willing to reopen the investigation without more evidence."

"What about Arianne?" Finn said.

"Can she really program?" Keiran said and winked. "Or do you have a thing for her?"

"I—I," Finn said. "I wouldn't deny that. But she's good. Yeah, no joke. What she did requires a deep level of understanding, otherwise BBTrey would've crashed right after. Ha ha."

Keiran smiled. "Well, see if she can help," he said. "Let me get her a visitor's pass."

"Thanks."

"Just keep it quiet. She can't be seen here too often."

"I can do that. Got it."

21

"Hello?"

"Nikola?" Finn said.

"Yeah! That's me. How can I help you?" replied a voice with a casual and confident affectation.

"This is Finn. As I explained in my messages, I'm looking for a certain product that was featured at the expo. I believe you have some footage we're interested in. We'd like to buy your video clip for an advertisement we're developing."

"Okay," he said. "My prices have gone up. Also, I need a special mention on your website . . ." He went on a rant about journalists not being compensated adequately. Finn quickly messaged Keiran for ideas on how to tackle the journalist.

"No problem, we understand. We can talk money," Finn said. "But did you shoot anything leading up to what we saw in the news? We need the unedited version from your Bots4U footage."

"I might have. Let me look."

A bit of back-and-forth ensued during which Finn assured him about how the publicity would help his career immensely. Keiran walked by Finn's door. Finn gave him a thumbs-up and signaled him to sit in the chair next to him. The journalist agreed to send over some files. Finn and Keiran looked over the video.

"Is this your entire video from Bots4U's demo?" Finn asked.

"I believe so; now don't you go back on your word," he said.

"No, you don't have to worry about that," Finn said. Keiran signaled again. "Here's my team lead, Keiran. He'll take care of the payment."

Keiran got on the phone with the journalist and transferred the money. Finn played the video using his headphones. There was so much going on at the expo that the audio in the extra footage was a horrendous mishmash of human voices and digital noise.

Arianne was overjoyed that Finn asked for her help. She rushed over to ABJ to see the recently acquired video. Finn suggested that they go a few blocks down from ABJ to see a sound engineer. Tapes from the twentieth century hung on the walls of the dingy, windowless office in the basement. The equipment on the tables looked new, but there was ample dust everywhere. Finn looked around a bit while Arianne watched the big, burly sound engineer hook up a few pieces of hardware and a specialized amplifier. His breath was heavy and loud, and Arianne wondered if that would interfere with the audio. He applied all the filters in his arsenal to draw out coherent phrases as Finn and Arianne strained to pay attention. Some of the filters were for different languages.

Suddenly Arianne jumped up. She shouted, "There! There! Could you please go back a few seconds?"

Barely audible amid a whole lot of chatter, she heard, "Das ass."

"Who's saying that?" Finn said. "Who's saying 'das ass'?"

"According to my instruments, it's coming from sort of behind and to the right of the camera," the sound engineer said.

The more times they played it, the clearer it sounded.

"I was worried that was a useless video we bought," Finn said as they walked back to ABJ.

"Yeah," Arianne said. "I'm so glad it's part of the video. Nobody believed me."

"I did," Finn said.

"Thanks," Arianne said, looking into his eyes.

"Arianne! How're you doing? Been a long time!" said a lady in the lobby while coming forward and giving her a hug.

A couple more people recognized Arianne and inquired about her family.

"I'm sure it's tough," said one.

"Time heals. Give your mom our best," said another.

———

Armed with the filtered version of the audio, Finn and Arianne went to Keiran's office.

"You two look victorious," Keiran said.

Arianne smiled. "You've got to hear this," Finn said. He played the video they heard many times earlier. Only, this time, all the noise was gone expect for human voices.

"Wow," Keiran said, nodding. "If you'll excuse me, I have to have some conversations." He left the room.

"Can I peek in the room with the BBs?" Arianne said to Finn. She hadn't been back in that room since BBTrey went up in smoke.

"I'll have to get authorization," Finn said. "The room is monitored 24/7."

"Right!" Arianne said. "So there must be footage from the BB room just before my dad's BB. . . Can I take a look?"

"Yes, of course," Finn said. "But I'm pretty sure the team combed through the video footage and found nothing suspicious." He looked at her. "I'm sorry. I bet you want to see your dad."

"Oh no," Arianne said. "I was just wondering if I might see something that your team has missed."

"Sure, let me show you," Finn said. He led Arianne toward the middle of the building, not too far away from the BB room. "As you can imagine, there's tons of footage. We use this processor to access all video content, and the viewing screen is in that corner," he said, pointing to a low pedestal.

"Thanks," Arianne said, bending down and starting to type in instructions.

"Find me if you need anything," Finn said.

"That was a good start," Keiran said to Finn in the hallway.

"Yeah, she's looking at footage from the BB room now," said Finn proudly.

"Oh?"

"She just wanted to go over what Trey had said the last few days," Finn said with a shrug. "And yeah, not to worry. I applied all the identity masks. Nobody's personal details are at risk."

Arianne sat there staring at the video of the BBs. They all looked alike to her, and strangely static. In those moments when none of the maintenance staff, engineers, or scientists were in the room, it didn't even look real. Keiran looked in on her after a few hours.

"How's it going?"

"Yeah?" Arianne said, feeling like she woke up from a nap.

"Gets kind of monotonous, doesn't it?"

"For sure," Arianne said. "Are all the people in the videos still working here?"

"Most of them."

"Can we talk to whoever last saw my dad?"

"Uhhh . . . sure," Keiran said. "But we have to wait to find out where ABJ wants us to take the investigation. Let's not get ahead of ourselves and give anybody a reason to pull the plug completely on this. Isn't it getting late? How about we continue tomorrow?"

"Okay," Arianne said.

"Arianne, trust me. I'm pushing hard for this," he said. After all, it was the most anomalous occurrence in ABJ's history. Since the investigation had led nowhere, management wanted to move past the death of BBTrey and BBFiona. It wouldn't take much for them to slam the door.

"They're thinking in just one direction, Mom," Arianne said that evening. "They keep saying that there's no evidence of a data stream with my code making its way out from Dad's BB. They're convinced it was a glitch. I hope Keiran gets the approval for me to look deeper." She got herself a glass of water and sat at the table. "Unless I find something convincing, this will become a hush-hush activity relegated to off hours. I can't be seen much. I can't be heard. I understand Keiran's position, but . . ."

"What about the voice output? Didn't everybody hear it? There's no question it was from your code."

Arianne shrugged.

"Did Keiran or Finn recognize anyone in the video?"

Still thinking about the video from the BB room and what she saw of BBTrey's last few days, Arianne was puzzled. "Oh," she said. "You mean the one from the expo? Not really, they would have told me."

The very next day, Arianne was talking to Keiran in his office.

"No," Keiran said. "I'm afraid we don't know anyone in it. ABJ didn't attend the expo this year."

"Can I view the entire video from the expo again?" asked Arianne.

"Of course."

Back in the viewing room, she watched the journalist's footage. She was so desperate for a lead that many people in there looked familiar.

Finn popped by. "Any ideas?" he said.

"Do you recognize anybody?"

"Yeah, I know some of them."

Arianne's jaw dropped, and her eyes got big. "Who? Which one?"

"Uhh. . . . There's only a handful of them, right? On a strict schedule?" he said, walking into the room. "Ah, you're talking about the expo! No, don't know anybody there." Finn sat down. "Sorry, I thought you meant the BB room maintenance staff."

"The more I stare at the video, the more familiar the people are starting to look," Arianne said, her eyes still on the video.

"Really? Like, from around here? As far as I know, ABJ didn't send . . ."

Arianne felt the clouds parting, as though she'd just unscrambled letters to form a word.

"What if Dad *was* at the expo? I mean his BB? Either virtually or physically."

He leaned closer to her. "You mean . . . his BB is still alive right now, somewhere?" he said. "After all this time . . . uhh . . . I wouldn't think that . . ."

"It was Dad's voice, though? And nobody knew why the robot replied with that."

"No question that's Trey's voice," Finn said. "But I don't think we should expect—"

"I know," Arianne said. "Guess I got carried away. Can we see that bot?"

Finn called Bots4U. "Hello? So I saw your demonstration at the International Robotics Expo. Would it be possible to see your bot in action?"

"Do you have a model number or name?" asked customer service.

"The one demoed at the expo in Germany? We're willing to travel."

"Oh, I'm sorry; we don't have one to see in person. I can send you a link."

"We'd like to order several units," Finn said. "But as you can understand, we want to see it first."

"Please put in an online request, and someone will contact you."

"Is there someone I can talk to about it? Someone who knows the technology?"

"I'm sorry, not at this time.

The following morning, Finn went by Keiran's office.

"We need to get in touch with the Bots4U staff doing the demonstrations at the expo. Their customer service has no technical info."

"Where are you going with this?" asked Keiran, adjusting his smart glasses.

"So Arianne, er . . . actually *we* were wondering if some hardware or at least software from BBTrey could have been at the expo."

Keiran knit his brows. "From a completely fried BB that went up in smoke?" he said.

"I told her that. Not in so many words. Didn't know what to say."

Keiran's face softened. "She did want to talk to someone who worked in the BB room."

"They're all still with us, right?" Finn said.

"Except for Carlina. She retired."

"The redhead?"

"Yeah," Keiran said, putting his smart glasses on the table. "Between you and me, I'm having a hell of a time reminding people about BBTrey or BBFiona."

"I don't feel right abandoning her now," Finn said. "We'll see what the organizers of the expo can tell us. Last stop. After that, honestly, I'm all out of ideas."

Finn contacted the organizers of the International Robotics Expo in Germany. They were very matter-of-fact. They had a list of companies and marketing materials that they could send over. If Finn could wait a couple of months, they could send the list for next year's expo.

Finn explained to the guy that he wanted to hire the company that handled network traffic during the expo. "The network engineers managed a tremendous load from all corners of the world quite effectively for the expo. It was impressive. Would they be interested in another gig?"

"Sending you a contact," said the voice over the phone.

After he got off the phone with the organizer, Finn called Arianne. "Hello? Arianne? I got a contact for a network engineer at the expo that day. I was wondering if we can dig in and find something useful?"

"Sure, please send it."

"Would you be able to find out more from home? Without raising any suspicion out here?"

"Uhhh, yeah, yeah. I need to locate recordings of the expo's events, find a replication server that's easiest to hack into, identify network sockets used by Bots4U. I . . . uhhh . . . I'll get on it immediately."

"Wish I could help more, but please call me if it's about anything other than networking software," said Finn.

22

Over a few days, Ozzie mostly sat in front of his computer at home, fixated on the news from the International Robotics Expo. He called the management team he had met at Bots4U. All seemed normal. Pretending to be an old lady, he even put in an online request for a companion bot, the HoneyBot. It seemed to go through fine. "Our team will contact you." Losing track of time, he realized too late that he was supposed to go to the lab for a mentoring session. Although the entryway camera would recognize him all the same, he wasn't in the mood for jokes about his buzz cut and tan.

He received a text from Alex: **Feeling better?**

Kinda, he texted back.

Great quarter for us! You missed the celebrations! Got your wish! Don't be late to the investor's meeting tomorrow morning, Alex texted.

The next morning, a buzz on his wrist woke Ozzie up early. He got up and was getting ready when he received a message from Bots4U: **Sandra, we're sorry, but it's taking longer to handle requests for the model of companion bot you requested.** He stood staring blankly at the mirror.

Don't forget—nice clothes! Another text from Alex.

He leaned on the bathroom counter with both hands and exhaled. Then he picked himself up, got dressed, and went to work.

The large conference room at AmieBots was abuzz with chatter. Alex had long prepped him for this meeting with investors. Brimming with confidence and great expectations, Alex was walking in and out, working the room.

"Anybody seen Ozzie? Not here yet?" he asked.

Ozzie was sitting around the corner in a small workroom. This was his first time pitching to a group on his own. Alex had trusted him with the new line of robots he had started to build. AmieBots had had a very successful quarter. Ozzie rehearsed his pitch in his head. *Successful demo at the International Robotics Expo The arrangement with Bots4U to crank out more such companions We just need more funding to . . .* Taking a deep breath, he walked into the conference room. To his relief, he observed that instead of sitting around the semicircular table tracking him with their eyes, people were up and chatting in small groups. Ozzie quietly walked up to a woman.

"We need to talk. Urgently and privately," he whispered.

"Geez, Ozzie, I almost didn't recognize you. Where's my favorite wild hair? Sharp suit by the way," she whispered back as she got up and followed Ozzie out and down the hallway into a small huddle room. Ozzie quickly shut the door and turned toward her, struggling to find his words.

"Is everything fine? Are you okay?" she asked, stepping closer to him.

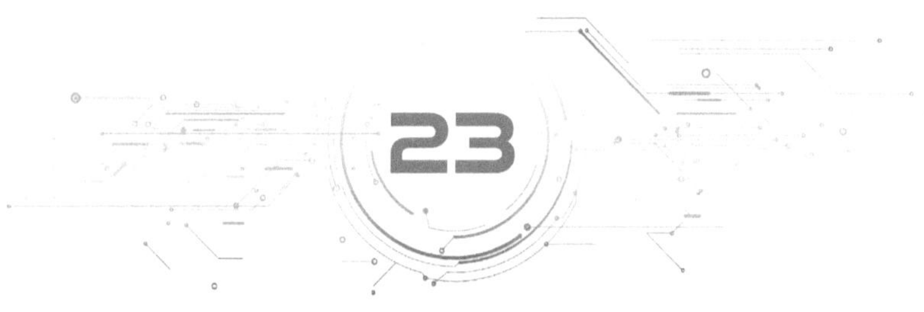

"**F**inn?" Arianne said over the phone. "Sorry to call you so late."

"It's all right," Finn said.

"I'm really not able to do much from home. You have a dedicated business tier connection to the internet that's faster and with access to more devices and nodes than the freeNet I have here."

"Sure . . .," Finn said.

"I can come by late tomorrow evening," Arianne said. "After most people leave?"

"Okay, around six then. Hang out by the street corner," Finn said. "I'll text you when the coast is clear."

"I'll pretend to be a jogger," Arianne said. "See you tomorrow."

A few minutes before six, Finn walked out of the lobby, pretended to have forgotten something, and went back into ABJ through the double doors at the front. **All clear**, he messaged Arianne. He almost didn't recognize her in workout clothes. He held the door open for her. She followed him quickly toward the back of ABJ into a barely used conference room with no windows. Arianne seemed strangely at ease. *Must be the clothes*, Finn thought. After a few hours of fidgeting in their chairs, swearing, and throwing up their hands in frustration, they managed to find the network and device addresses used by Bots4U during the international expo.

"It's almost nine, want to get something to eat?" Finn said.

"I heard your stomach growling earlier," Arianne said and smiled. "Let's go."

They both made a quick trip out and then got back into the weeds. They pored through logs to see which devices were active using the time stamp from the video the journalist sent. Having started slouching in his chair for a couple of hours now, Finn was almost horizontal. Arianne kept alternating her hands to prop her head up.

Finn sat up suddenly. "I wonder if the security folks are here; they're sure to look in if they see activity on the cameras." He peeked into the hallway. "How about we pick it back up tomorrow? We can save a snapshot of everything."

"But every moment counts. What if one of the devices goes off-line? We'd lose everything," Arianne pleaded. "I have a feeling we're almost there. We're on the verge of finding something big."

"You said that a few times already," Finn said with a smile. "We'd draw a great deal of attention if people start coming in to work and discover that we've been cybertracing all night. We'd really lose everything, including your access to this place."

They dispersed as the sun was bubbling up on the horizon.

Having spent a couple of evenings cybertracing, Finn was getting tired of staying up with Arianne all night in addition to getting his work done during the day.

"Wish I could do this during the day. Couldn't we convince them to reopen the investigation?" Finn said, dropping his voice and leaning over Keiran's desk.

"Ha! How exactly do you propose I explain illegal hacking off hours using ABJ's domain?" Keiran said with his brows raised.

"We have network and device addresses used by Bots4U," Finn said to Keiran. "Finding the bot from the expo shouldn't take long from here."

"You sure? Or is that sleep deprivation talking?"

"I guess both," Finn said and slumped down on a chair. "I've had to catch up on the latest cybertracing techniques, too."

"Impressive!" Keiran said. "But hate to say this, we need more than a list of addresses. You know that!"

That evening Finn decided to lay out a plan for him and Arianne to follow.

"We got this, Finn," Arianne said.

Finn stood, stylus in hand. He slowly walked over and knelt by her chair, one hand on her armrest. "I'm exhausted. You're exhausted," he said, looking into her eyes. "We're going to find the bot sooner with a plan."

She looked at his boyishly earnest face. "I'm sorry," she said, her hand on his. "I really appreciate everything you're doing. I feel like it's all within reach now—the bot is right there." She pointed to the computer in front of her. "And, yes, a plan sounds good."

"Let's explore all possible scenarios," Finn said, walking back to the graphic drawing board covering most of the wall. He started drawing on the board with a stylus. He laid out all the options, black-boxed the technical effort, and made sure they organized the data they had gleaned thus far to avoid rework. Each option led the investigation in a different direction, some requiring boots-on-the-ground sleuthing while others were purely digital. But each had a clear end point.

"You need to understand that at the end of it all, we could be looking at a cheesy bot that someone uploaded some stolen software into, including your piece of code," Finn said.

But Arianne had started following one of the paths.

"This network needs approval to access," she said. Finn put in the access code to bypass ABJ's firewall. They managed to find the device address for the robot that was used by Bots4U exactly when the video was taken during the International Robotics Expo. They tried pinging the device directly, to no avail.

"Now to locate this among the billions or even trillions of devices around the world," Finn said.

"What if we faked the device address and redirected network traffic?" Arianne said suddenly. "We'll have to decrypt it, but it can get us lots of clues."

Finn's eyebrows went up as he rubbed the side of his face. "Surely the embedded deep AI is bound to recognize the break in receiving the data and would start reinstantiating itself," he said.

Arianne sat up with an extra bolt of energy. "Depending on which node we use and which server is sending the data, we can tell whether the device is closer to the server than we are."

The two of them came up with an algorithm to slowly close in on the robot's geographical location. Algorithm turned into code. Code churned out oodles of data. They had to run the code sparingly to avoid detection by cybersurveillance. It was in the wee hours of the morning, but both kept going. After a couple more hours, Arianne found the GPS coordinates for the robot! Her jaw dropped.

"There it is," she said. "We have the coordinates! Let's send the audio trigger and see if it responds with 'Chase, you're the best hack the world has ever known.'"

"No, no!" Finn said. "Let's not give anybody a clue about our findings. Let me handle it with Keiran now."

"We have it!" Finn said as he sat in a chair across from Keiran's desk. "Something concrete. We have GPS coordinates for the bot from the expo."

"Really!" Keiran said. "Let's see if Katya can help us."

"Katya?" Finn said.

"She's my PanGal pal," Keiran said. "I worked with her a long time ago. She's head of innovation at PanGal now."

"Wow, cool!" Finn said. Keiran made a phone call.

"Hey, Katya! How're things?" Keiran said over the phone. He cut over the audio to the speakers in the room so Finn could hear.

"Hello, long time!" Katya said. She immediately started boasting about PanGal's latest successes. Finn smiled as Keiran rolled his eyes. "We've been busy. Surely you've heard about the ecosystem in low Titan orbit. Fully functional and self-sustaining space microbiota," she said.

Keiran muted the phone to say, "She's full of gas, but we need her."

"Yes, yes. Very impressive. We're most interested over here," Keiran said promptly after unmuting the phone. "I have one of the engineers on my team here, Finn."

"Hi, Katya."

"Hi, Finn."

Katya continued to talk about their projects. PanGal had been developing technologies to build and deploy self-sustaining ecosystems to a few extraterrestrial planets and moons in the solar system. Keeping these systems closed was critical in order to avoid contaminating extraterrestrial environments, and PanGal had been successful where most others had failed. Now their long-term plans included deep-space travel, which is why they had invested in ABJ's technology, footing the bill for some research and services. When she had finished, he reeled off the story about the investigation into BBTrey to her.

"So we could follow this lead all the way around the world to a children's toy?" Katya said and chuckled.

"Something fishy is going on," Finn said.

"I don't want to oversell this opportunity, but we need your help," Keiran said. "Remember the case of the BBs that got electrocuted some time back?"

"Yes, yes, I do," she said. "A freak short in the circuitry fried them?"

"Right," Keiran said.

"So what exactly do you need from us?"

"For starters, do you have someone close to the location who can verify that this device exists? Some sleuthing work?"

"A detective and a few thugs," joked Finn.

Keiran quickly said, "What he means is—"

"I know what he means," she said. "This is going to be very expensive and risky."

"Well, Katya, I've always admired you for the risks you guys take. Look where it's led PanGal." He winked at Finn.

"Hiro was the cybersleuth we used last time. Let me see if he's available."

"Finn can work with him," Keiran said. "Perhaps he can fill in for one of the thugs."

"He insists on using his own thugs," she said with a laugh. "All right, we'll come by to meet you both next week."

The next week, Finn poked his head into Keiran's office. "They're in the lobby," he said from the hallway, looking at his wristband.

Keiran nodded, got up, and joined Finn.

Katya wore her long, blonde, flowing hair flamboyantly. Hiro, by contrast, kept it minimal; he could disappear in a crowd of well-dressed college students. Introductions were made, and the four retreated to a conference corner in the lobby. The conference corner was a physically open space with acoustics and white-noise emitters designed for privacy. Hiro immediately got down to business—he was very professional.

"I don't want all the details, just enough to do my job." He took a quick glance at Katya. "Not sure if you've told them. I understand you need access to a device in Japan."

"I wouldn't say 'access,'" Finn said. "But we need to confirm that it has a piece of software we're looking for."

"Okay," Hiro said. "So I can hack digital locks and passwords to get you physical access to the device and set up a cybershield to warp outgoing signals, or incoming if that's what you need. I usually bring two bodyguards. They have everything we'll need as far as an invisibility cloak. And also for physical protection, of course. It would depend on how many of you are going to be there."

Keiran raised his eyebrows at Finn. Katya flicked her hair back and stifled a yawn.

Finn said to Keiran, "Time would be of the essence. I'll need a couple of people from our team, at least one for sure."

"If you can briefly walk us through your team's process," Keiran said.

"Looks like you can work this out between yourselves," Katya said and got up to leave. She raised an eyebrow. "Exciting! Keep me up-to-date."

Hiro explained that he would first reach out to his global team to make sure the GPS location he was given was legitimate. He expected to hear back in the affirmative with a list of devices at the location that should include the device address of interest given to him by Finn. Next, he would do as much digital snooping as possible. Actual boots on the ground would reveal the final bits of information needed for the raid. His team would surveil the location according to the kind of building it was and what kind of access was available. A high-rise apartment building in the middle of the city, with good security measures, would require many days of discreet observation. He said Keiran's team would come in after he laid out a plan for how to get access to the device in question with the least amount of risk to everybody involved, including the current presumed owner of the said device. He would be there personally with Keiran's team.

"I'll send you specifics on the location of the device and how much time we need," Finn said. "Also, I'd say it's going to be myself and another person coming along."

"All right," Keiran said.

Hiro nodded and left.

Walking back from the lobby, Keiran leaned closer to Finn.

"Is Arianne game?" he said. "Her family can't know."

"Uhh . . . ," Finn said. "Haven't asked her yet. I assume she'd want to."

Arianne received a call. "Hi, Finn." She listened quietly for a while as Finn went through their conversation with Hiro.

"Keiran wasn't sure if you'd go," Finn said, "since you can't tell anyone about it."

"Would I ever!" Arianne said. "Thanks for including me in this."

"No, Arianne," Finn said. "This is yours. We wouldn't have come this far without you. I'll let you know as soon as I hear from Hiro."

A couple of days later, Keiran and Finn received a message from Hiro. "We have everything we need from our end. Ready to coordinate with your team."

Finn asked Arianne to rush to ABJ. He led her to the familiar conference room in the back with no windows. The two of them sat on tall stools. Finn made a video call to Hiro. Hiro appeared on the screen across the table from Arianne and Finn.

"Hiro, this is Arianne," Finn said. Arianne and Hiro said hello to each other. To Finn's right was the digital drawing board. "So I was trying to sketch it out." He stood up with a stylus.

"May I?" Hiro said as he took control of the board. He pasted in a 3D sketch of an apartment in a high-rise building. There were arrows marked for himself and the bodyguards. There were separate arrows for Arianne and Finn. "I'll send this to you both. Remember to tell your family that you're going to a bioelectronics conference for landing gigs, leapfrogging careers, whatever. No one else needs to know anything. Questions?"

"Not at this time," Arianne said.

"I'll send you step-by-step instructions as soon as you land in Tokyo," Hiro said and hung up.

"I don't think I'll have much time to pack," Arianne said, getting up.

"Again, we really don't know what we're getting into," Finn said.

Keiran peeked in. "All set with Hiro?" he said.

"That's about all that's set," Finn said. "We have no idea what to expect there."

"That's why it's called an investigation," Keiran said, tapping Finn on his shoulder.

"I was just saying that we could see a child's toy, as Katya was joking," Finn said, "or nothing of interest—maybe a toaster oven! So no preconceived notions, no expectations." He looked at Arianne.

"But the first priority is your safety. Just follow Hiro's instructions carefully," Keiran said.

"And make sure we don't get caught," Arianne said, still excited.

"That's not nearly as important as your safety," Keiran said. "Keep me up-to-date at least a couple of times a day. Let me put it this way—you can never send me too many messages." He gave Arianne and Finn a reassuring pat on the back. "Go get some sleep."

Arianne was getting prepared for the trip. Hiro had said that she needed just two pairs of clothes—he'd arrange for special "raid wear." She went in and out of her room, looking for a bag and her hairbrush and mostly just wondering what to pack. *Raid wear*, she thought and, for the first time, realized that what she was about to do wasn't exactly legal.

"Mom? Where's the stuff I put in the dry-cleaning cabinet yesterday?" she called.

Val was somewhere downstairs. "Your blue pantsuit? And the short skirt?" she said.

"Never mind. Found them. Thanks," Arianne said.

"Make sure you take that pantsuit," Val said. "You look very nice in it."

I better take it, Arianne thought. She stuffed it into the bag.

As she was packing her toiletries, she tipped a bottle of body lotion on the bath counter. She tried to grab it before it headed into the sink. The bottle slid off her hand and hit the floor with a loud crash.

Momentarily Val appeared at Arianne's doorway. "Sweetie, with all that's happening, if this isn't a good time, you don't have to go," she said. "There will be plenty of opportunities later."

"It's all right, Mom. It will take my mind off of things," Arianne said.

Chase had also followed the sound of shattering glass. "Can I chaperone?" he said, hanging on the door. "I've never been to Tokyo."

"Sure! Why not bring Misha along?" Arianne smiled with a wink.

25

Having flown thousands of miles from home, following Hiro's messages, Arianne and Finn waited at a fairly busy eating area at the airport for further instructions. Arianne kept tapping her feet. She put her glasses on. Her eyes lingered on the virtual translation that hovered above the Japanese emergency exit sign.

Finn followed her eyes.

"Just wondering what is behind that door," she said.

Eventually Hiro appeared. He said something in Japanese, pointing to a chair.

"Yes, sure," Arianne said. Hiro seemed smaller than he appeared over the video phone. Finn was fumbling with his glasses that would translate what Hiro was going to say.

"You don't need those," Hiro said in a low voice. "Assume you're being watched and recorded. The best cover for you two is a couple vacationing together."

"Yes, understood," Finn said. Arianne nodded.

"Just follow my instructions, and we all should be safe," Hiro said. "I shouldn't be seen interacting with you in public until the raid. Messaging is fine. Use my encryption software for all messaging." He gave them each a handwritten piece of paper with two addresses. "When I message you, you're going to be taking a pod to the first address. And then you're going to walk to the second address. The back of the paper has a hand-drawn map. Don't enter the second address into any device. Remember, you're visiting a friend there. Go ahead and enjoy touring the city until one p.m." Finn leaned back in his chair. Arianne remained stiff. "I mean that," Hiro said, casually looking around. "It's a beautiful city. Lots to do. I summoned a pod for you. Just step out through the main entrance. Now, let's split." He got up. "Oh, and here's lunch," he said, handing over a bento box. "Eat in your hotel room."

"Thank you," Arianne said. "I've heard so much about these."

Once outside, Arianne and Finn started receiving messages from the pod. Finn replied with the address of the hotel. They got on the pod and were going through the streets of Tokyo.

"It's so clean," Arianne said.

"Yeah," Finn said, looking out the windows. "And they don't allow business names or any kind of signs to be visible on the outside of buildings." He put on his smart glasses to see what the buildings and landmarks were.

"Wow," Arianne said. She put on her smart glasses, too. "It's pretty without ugly signage." She took in the sights for a while. "I thought it was a crowded city. Pod 1251A?" Arianne said. "How has the population of Tokyo changed over the past few decades?"

After reeling off some numbers, the pod said, "With ultrafast transportation and mandatory staggering of business schedules according to location, the city optimally spreads foot and vehicle traffic throughout the day to minimize bottlenecks."

Momentarily, the pod stopped and announced, "Aoyama Hotel."

They got off and went through the lobby.

"Let's see," Finn said. "We're on floor six, room D four." Arianne showed her wristband to the sensor on the elevator.

Arianne and Finn freshened up and opened up the bento box. There were two wigs, a beard for Finn, and heel inserts for Arianne. Finn tried the beard on. Arianne almost fell down laughing.

"Looks like you're playing dress-up," she said. "I'm sorry, I didn't mean . . ." She instinctively hugged him tight. "Thank you so much for doing this."

Finn rubbed her back. "Of course," he said.

"Gosh, I needed that," Arianne said. "Was that just for comic relief?"

"No," he said, looking at a handwritten sheet of instructions. "We're going to wear these after stepping out of the pod at the first address."

"Oh," Arianne said.

"Now we need something to eat," he said. They walked to a bakery nearby. After lunch, they strolled around taking pictures.

Then the messages started arriving from Hiro about the raid: **All's well. How're you two enjoying the city? Summon a pod to get to A1.**

On their way to the first address, Arianne slipped the heel inserts into her boots while on the pod. They got off and discreetly put on the wigs and beard. They pretended to take pictures per Hiro's instructions. **Walk over,** Hiro's message said. Arianne and Finn walked over to the second address and took the elevator to the fourth floor to "visit their friend." They were still on the elevator when Hiro messaged again. **Entered apartment. Proceed swiftly to apt #5A3.**

"Excuse me," Finn said as they went past a couple of huge men carrying a large table right next to the open door. Hiro was already in the apartment. He quickly closed the door behind Arianne and Finn.

"I just deployed the cybershield," Hiro said. "No communication between the apartment and the outside world. It's all yours now." He kept a lookout through the window.

Arianne and Finn spun their gaze around the apartment. The living room was large, with tasteful modern furniture and a couple of plants by the window.

"Das ass, das ass," Arianne called out.

"Chase, you're the best hack the world has ever seen. Chase, you're the best hack the world has ever seen." The voice came from a cute but common-looking bot in the corner right by the entrance to the kitchen.

"That's the bot from the video," Arianne said. "Dad! Dad, it's me!" she screamed and leaped forward.

"Arianne, we can't tear anything down now—can't leave a trace," Finn said as he held Arianne back from ripping off the outer shell of the bot. "It's just a piece of software in there that's responding. We're here to get as many clues that trace back to . . ." Finn started running some diagnostics from his phone and trying to communicate with the bot.

"Hey! There's a lot of chatter bouncing between this and another device inside the apartment, right here," Arianne said, looking over his shoulder.

"Well, we've all been trying to talk to it?" Finn said.

"No, it's not something any of us is doing," Arianne said. She kept probing around the bot.

Finn looked quite puzzled. "Is the owner still here?" he gasped at Hiro.

"Not at all. She's not. We have eight and a half minutes left until she gets back. She's gone for a walk as usual," Hiro replied, still keeping watch out of the window.

"Who's the bot communicating with?" Finn said. He and Arianne hurried around the apartment, wildly searching. "Could there be another bot? Working in parallel? Like a twin?"

"Or is this just the face with the main unit someplace else?" Arianne said, thinking aloud.

Finn swung open a door. He and Arianne stood staring into a tiny room the size of a small closet with an elaborate setup like in a laboratory. "What the—*damn*! Hiro? How much time do we have?" he yelled.

"How much do you need? Would we still need to be back?" asked Hiro.

Arianne and Finn frantically followed the mess of conduits and hardware. Finn saw a lens mounted at about eye level and looking down from the corner. He picked up a small bag lying around and threw it on for cover. Arianne soon noticed a box on a low pedestal on the floor. She reached down, opened it, gasped, and about fainted upon seeing the contents, which looked like a completely intact BB.

"It must be Dad!" Arianne said, standing motionless, looking at Finn. "Dad? Dad?" Arianne collapsed on her knees beside the box.

Finn quickly put his arm around Arianne. He examined the BB from a few angles without touching it.

"It's gotta be one of ours," Finn said.

"Why isn't he responding?" Arianne said.

"Seems to have been outfitted with some identity-masking filters. No doubt heavily customized. It's getting input only from the sensors on the bot out there," Finn said, pointing to the living room.

"We have to take him back and take all the modifications off," Arianne said.

"Thirty seconds," Hiro called out.

"How can we leave him here?" Arianne said.

"We'll have to come back prepared to maintain the BB all the way back home," said Finn.

They rushed to take full stock of the setup, snap pictures, and gather as much information and evidence as possible. As soon as the two of them stepped out of the apartment, Hiro disabled the cybershield, locked the door, and retreated nimbly into the hallway. He motioned to them to walk on ahead while he turned around, walked the other way, and disappeared around the corner.

The two huge men moving a table appeared again. Right in front of Arianne and Finn, the table was folded in a couple of seconds like it was made of paper, and one of the men tucked it into a small bag. As they turned around and walked past, one of them said, "I'm sorry, are you looking for the elevator? Take a right here and then all the way down to the end of the hallway. By the pictures on the wall, yeah?"

Arianne pulled Finn's arm and hurried to do as the man said, whispering, "Bodyguards," into his ear.

Take all gear off before entering elevator, Hiro's message said.

26

"You mean an intact BB—one of ours?" Keiran said on the phone. He was incredulous.

"Yes. Totally rigged," Finn said. "The research behind it appears sophisticated. Quite impressive. Someone else is involved here. Not a job for a cheesy company like Bots4U." He was almost whispering, although he and Arianne were in the hotel room.

"This is great work!" Keiran said.

"Wish I could take all the credit. Arianne came up with the missing piece of the puzzle, yet again."

"Remarkable!" Keiran said, and then added in a more serious tone, "also distressing. Obviously there's a breach here we need to plug. But let's first get both of you and the BB back home safe."

"The last thing we want is to lose the BB on the way back," Finn said. "It's the only thing we need for the investigation at this point." He started reeling off the myriad ways the BB could stop functioning and how the long journey might affect the chemistry.

"Wait," Keiran said. "Bots4U has transported the BB several times. Clearly they've achieved a level of robustness and mobility. You've done great; don't doubt yourself now. Using all your footage and pictures, we'll send a couple of people with all the equipment you need for the trip home."

"We need to rush," Arianne said. "It's only a matter of time before Bots4U finds out and reports us to the authorities."

"If there's some shady business Bots4U is into," Keiran said, "which is my guess, they're not going to involve the authorities."

"Can Hiro's team make it look like a random burglary?" Finn said.

"Hiro's team will do what they did on the first raid," Keiran said. "Radu from Hardware—Finn, you know him—is going over tomorrow morning. His team has packed all the equipment you need into one suitcase. He'll deliver it to your room. Head directly to the airport after the raid. Text Radu as soon as you reach the airport."

"Airport?" Arianne said.

"Yes, to hand over the suitcase," Keiran said.

"Oh," Arianne said and heaved a sigh of relief. "Thanks."

"Of course," Keiran said. "He'll know how to get it through security."

"See you soon," Finn said.

"Be safe," Keiran said.

Arianne and Finn strolled through a garden the following morning.

"Do you think the lady who owned the bot suspects anything?" said Arianne.

"I doubt it," Finn said. "What're the odds she was trying to talk to her bot when Hiro used the cybershield?"

"Wouldn't the bot record or report it?" Arianne said as she bent over some fragrant yellow flowers.

"Someone has to go digging in there first," Finn said. "Besides, Hiro did use some scrambling software, so that should help."

Finn messaged Hiro: **How would we know if the lady cried havoc and Bots4U took the bot away?**

24/7 surveillance, Hiro messaged back.

Shortly, they received a message from Hiro: **Dinner plans. Package delivered to your room.**

"He's sending us dinner?" Arianne said.

"He likes being cryptic," Finn said. "Bet it's like the bento box he gave us yesterday."

Back in the hotel room, they opened the package to find a beige evening gown and a navy blazer. According to instructions, they were to be worn on top of their regular clothes. Included was the address for the restaurant.

Hiro messaged again: **Leave at 5:30. It's one of those upscale restaurants with actual human waitstaff. Have an elaborate dinner, four course . . . seven course . . . we just need you to be on standby.**

The two of them showed up at the restaurant, Finn with the suitcase in one hand. The restaurant was situated on the thirty-fifth floor overlooking the city; the view through the glass walls was spectacular. They were ushered to a table. Finn put the suitcase under the table.

"You look . . . breathtaking," Finn said, hesitating and shifting his eyes as they sat down. "I . . . I meant to say that earlier."

With her head full of details on the clandestine operation ahead of them, Arianne stared blankly for a second before blushing nervously. She was about to reciprocate with a compliment when a waiter appeared.

"What can I get miss started on? You, sir?" Finn heard the translation with his smart glasses.

Arianne looked up from her messages and almost knocked a glass off the table.

"Something to drink?" Finn said to her. She put her smart glasses on.

"Perhaps a little drink to relax first? Are we celebrating an occasion? May I suggest . . ." The waiter pointed to the list of beverages projected onto Arianne's place mat.

"I'll try the appetizer drink, with . . . ginger. But go light on the ginger, please," Arianne said as casually as possible. Then she smiled and made some small talk about how appetizers are a misnomer.

"I'll have the same," Finn said, quickly scanning the menu on his place mat.

Through their dinner, Arianne and Finn kept receiving messages from Hiro.

The lady did not leave the apartment as scheduled. Waiting.

Okay. Plan B. Wrap up dinner.

"My flight just got rescheduled. We'll need to leave," Finn said to the waiter.

Leave right now. Summoned a pod for you. Tear off formal wear, hand over to bodyguard in the pod.

Don't wait for bodyguard. Head straight to apt.

Arianne and Finn blew into the apartment shortly after Hiro dodged surveillance devices, picked digital locks, and deployed cybershields. A lady was lying on the sofa. Hiro threw a cybercloak on the bot. Finn and Arianne hurried into the small room. Arianne switched the BB with the dummy in the suitcase that Finn was carrying. She and Finn hooked up the conduits from the BB, matching their colors to sockets in the suitcase. As they left, Hiro administered the antidote to the tranquilizer that he had given the lady. Arianne and Finn rushed to the airport. Once there, Finn sent a message to Radu. Radu appeared seemingly out of nowhere, smiled, tapped Finn on the shoulder, and took the suitcase away.

"Was that him? Did you recognize him?" Arianne said.

"Yeah, no worries," Finn said. "That's him."

27

"Arianne! You're back early. How was the event? Chase and I were about to—Oh. Hi, Finn!" Val said.

Arianne collapsed on the sofa in the living room.

"Hi, Mrs. Primeson," Finn said.

"Is everything okay?" Val said, alternating her gaze from one to the other.

Arianne and Finn explained everything. Val sat down and listened as if she had seen a ghost.

"We won't know what state he's in until all the modifications are undone," Arianne said.

Early the following day, Arianne went to ABJ. Finn and Keiran had been working on the retrieved BB with a team of engineers, neuralware experts, and neurochemists. They had been uninstalling filters and undoing the rerouting of sensors.

"Did they actually modify . . . him?" Arianne said. "As in, is he a different person with his memory completely replaced?"

"We're about to find out," Keiran said. "I didn't want to say anything earlier. That could possibly be irreversible."

"When can he communicate?" asked Arianne.

"Trust me, Arianne, that's the first consideration here," Keiran said.

After a moment, one of the engineers exclaimed, "I got in! I got in!"

"Can he see us? Can he hear us?" Arianne rushed close to the BB.

"Uhhh not yet. I don't think so," said the engineer.

Trey? Is it you in there? the engineer fed into the BB's digital input port.

Yes! It's me! Trey Primeson, came the answer.

The whole room erupted as they all crowded around the one engineer "talking" to BBTrey.

BBTrey responded: **I've been trying to get someone's attention. Nobody seemed to hear me.**

"Can you ask him if he remembers anything from what happened?" Keiran said.

BBTrey responded: **Carlina. Ozzie. AmieBots. I have been chanting the three names so I don't forget.**

"The filters that were installed by the crooks blocked him," said the neuralware expert.

Arianne, Finn, and Keiran pieced the story together.

"So the freak short in the BB never happened?"

"It did. It happened to the dummy that was switched for the stolen BB."

"That's a lot of trouble and risk to take."

"What's better than the actual human brain for true human personality and authenticity encapsulated as a companion bot?"

"Humor, sarcasm, and cunning are some of the hardest traits to engineer."

"What about the second BB that could still be out there? BBFiona?"

ABOUT THE AUTHOR

S. L. HEMM has always been intrigued by the endless potential of virtual reality. Hemm's background in engineering and technology led to musings about our mortality, how manifestations of our existence could linger on in the cybercloud, and where VR technology could lead humanity in the very near future, sometimes taking ominous turns.